Praise for the Clockwork Witch Series

Intriguing magic, gender politics, and historical detail weave together in this coming-of-age fantasy debut [...] Readers will especially enjoy Sonnier's inventive worldbuilding.
– Publisher's Weekly

The Clockwork Witch takes a fun, familiar premise and goes the extra mile into making it something novel. I was impressed with the amount of worldbuilding and characterization in this story and found myself hoping for a sequel. Perhaps if we're lucky, we'll get one in the future.
– SFRevu

A vibrant and fast-moving tale that melds steampunk and magic to great effect. I look forward to following Arabella and company into the next book.
– Madison Public Library

Other eSpec Books titles by
Michelle D. Sonnier

THE CLOCKWORK WITCH SERIES
The Clockwork Witch
An Unceasing Hunger
(forthcoming)

Other eSpec Books titles including
Michelle D. Sonnier

After Punk:
Steampowered Tales of the After Life

Death's Embrace

Michelle D. Sonnier

eBooks

Pennsville, NJ

PUBLISHED BY
eSpec Books LLC
Danielle McPhail,
Publisher
PO Box 242,
Pennsville, New Jersey 08070
www.especbooks.com

ISBN: 978-1-949691-11-5
ISBN (ebook): 978-1-949691-10-8

Interior Design: Danielle McPhail
www.Sidhenadaire.com

Images - http://www.fotolia.com
Interior Graphic: Raven © rin
Section Break: Peerless Decorative Feather © irinakrivoruchko
Illustrations: © Ed Coutts
1 - Macaria and the Death Cards
2 - Stephan attacks Joanna

Cover Art: Vladimir Sazonov, http://www.shutterstock.com
Double exposure portrait of young woman and pine with black crow.
Double exposure portrait of young woman and blooming branch of the apple.

Cover Design: Mike McPhail
Copyediting: Greg Schauer

Dedicated to

Jhada

for sharing knowledge about a good death.
There is much of you in Joanna.

Contents

Death's Embrace

Chapter One

Poland, 1771

In hindsight, Macaria saw that spring as a new beginning rather than an ending, but at the time it felt like the world was crashing down around her ears. The winter had been especially harsh that year, the snow holding on longer than anyone predicted and the foodstuffs in the root cellars all over town dwindled far below levels anyone was comfortable with. That year, for the first time in Macaria's memory, there were whispered grumbles about the tithes due to the local hedgewitch, her mother.

Macaria's mother, Elzbieta, worked hard to ingratiate herself to the people of their little hamlet as she did every winter. It was within a village's rights to ask for a new hedgewitch from the Polish Council of Witches if they believed their current one was too old, lazy, or incompetent. No appointment from the Council guaranteed a lifetime of work, but this appointment had been her mother's first, and they both liked the village. Her mother confided that she hoped it would become a hereditary appointment that Macaria would inherit. So Elzbieta went out through deep snows and howling winds to deliver tinctures and poultices, often bringing sickness upon herself. Her stores of healing herbs dropped shockingly low for such an industrious hedgewitch as herself. Macaria and Elzbieta looked for the spring just as eagerly, if not more so than the people of the town.

"Do I have to go?" Macaria winced at the whine in her own voice.

"Yes, you must go," Mama said as she fixed her daughter with a gimlet stare. "You will not bring shame on the Niemiera line by abandoning your ritual duties just because you do not wish to muddy your shoes."

"I haven't even blossomed yet, Mama, I'm not even considered an official part of the house," Macaria muttered as she stared down at her feet. "And they are very nice shoes."

Mama lifted Macaria's chin with her forefinger and met her gaze. "There is plenty of time for you to blossom yet, sweetling. You are not quite thirteen and your blood is not yet upon you. You must go."

Macaria's mother dropped her hand and turned to put a basket on her hip to go collect the wizened carrots and turnips from the root cellar for their supper.

"You can wear my shoes for the ritual if it bothers you that much," she called over her shoulder. "I don't mind cleaning the good mud of the ritual from my clothes."

Macaria winced again at her mother's tone but she also breathed a sigh of relief. She immediately scampered up the ladder to the small loft to dig out an extra pair of socks from her clothes chest at the foot of her bed. Mama's feet were still bigger than her own even though Macaria had almost reached the height of a full-grown woman already.

Elzbieta rummaged through her small box of treasures while Macaria stood by the door, impatiently shifting her weight from foot to foot. Without looking up Elzbieta murmured, "Be still, child. Learning patience and stillness will serve you well when the time comes to start your spellcasting lessons."

"If I ever get to have spellcasting lessons," Macaria muttered as she rolled her eyes.

This time Elzbieta looked up at her daughter with a frown. "Of course, you'll get to have spellcasting lessons, why ever wouldn't you?"

"Not everyone in our line is a witch, Mama," Macaria said with a sigh. "And it is getting late for me. Maybe I am destined to be mundane."

"Bite your tongue," Elzbieta grumbled as she returned to her treasure box. "Aha! Here it is!"

Elzbieta produced a beautiful strand of pale yellow polished beads that sparkled and glowed in the thin sunlight spilling in through the recently opened windows. At last, the air ceased to be bitter and held a faint breath of spring. Everyone in the village threw open their doors and windows that morning with sighs of relief.

"Citrine," Elzbieta said. "Naturally encourages growth and renewal, and discourages negative energy, but this strand bears enhancement spells to make those natural tendencies even stronger."

"Those are so beautiful, Mama," Macaria breathed in an awestruck whisper. "Why would you want to sacrifice them to Marzanna?"

"Why would I want to sacrifice them to Marzanna?" Elzbieta threw her hands up in exasperation. "Do you want to live through another winter like the one we just had? Sacrifices that hurt bring more benefit. Perhaps if I give this to Marzanna we will be blessed with a bountiful spring and summer, and then have a more gentle winter." She cradled the beads in her palms for just a moment, caressing them with one last fond look before she pressed them into her daughter's hands and closed Macaria's fingers over them.

"Don't forget to tell Marzanna where they came from," Elzbieta said. "And be respectful. And on your way back watch for where Lady's Mantle and mint might be returning. I'm especially low on those." Elzbieta kissed her daughter on both cheeks and sent her on her way.

Even with an extra pair of socks, Mama's shoes were still a little loose on Macaria's feet. As she tromped to the center of town where the ritual was to begin, she hoped that she would not get any blisters. Her back ached and she was tired, and she wished her mother hadn't been so firm about her attending the regular springtime ritual of drowning Marzanna. She paused for a moment to stretch and rub the small of her back.

With a sigh and a shake of her head, she continued on. She reached into her apron pocket and fingered the beads her mother gave her. For a moment, she considered keeping them for herself, not giving them to Marzanna as her mother instructed. They were so pretty and if her powers never blossomed they would look lovely with her best dress as she tried to lure in a husband. But if her powers did blossom she wouldn't need a husband; witches were free to marry or not as they chose. And if she didn't gift the beads as instructed it was just as likely the energy would turn on her. Her mother did say they had been spelled. They weren't just plain beads. Who knew how that might rebound on her? Macaria sighed and pulled her hand out of her pocket. Best to stay away from the temptation.

By the time Macaria reached the center of town the village children had already dressed the effigy in cast-off clothes from the village women. The gray wool dress with the ragged hem looked just like one that belonged to the miller's wife. The bright red, much-patched apron had surely belonged to Old Agnes, and the green silk scarf wrapped around the effigy's head just as obviously came from the town headman's wife. She had bragged about it so when he brought it back to her from Krakow when he went there on town business. The older boys were preparing to hoist Marzanna up on the pole they would use to carry her through town to the river. Macaria started to run.

"Wait! Wait!" she cried as she trotted up the cluster of children and young people gathered around the effigy of Marzanna. "I have one more thing," she panted, out of breath.

The boys nodded and held out the effigy. All around her, the young folk laughed and sang, taking joy in the air finally feeling soft again, without the sharp tang of winter. In spite of her misgivings about coming, Macaria couldn't help but feel her spirit lift with the infectious happiness.

"Bright blessings," said the nearest boy, just two years older than herself, twinkling blue eyes peering out from under a shock of black hair. "Your gift can only make it better." He smiled shyly and Macaria smiled just as shyly back. If she were to take a husband, she could do worse than Aleksy, son of the blacksmith, with his strong hands and quiet ways.

Macaria pulled the beads from her pocket and fastened them around Marzzana's neck with trembling fingers. The jubilance hushed as everyone strained to see what kind of blessing the daughter of the village witch conferred on Marzanna. Macaria frowned. She hated being the center of attention.

"These are from me and my mother, Marzanna," Macaria mumbled under her breath as her cheeks burned bright. "Please be kind to us." She stepped back and shoved both hands into her apron pockets, giving the boys a jerky nod.

They hoisted the effigy up with a cheer and started twirling in circles. The boys let out a few piercing whistles. Macaria's smile began to creep up again as she allowed herself to drift back toward the edges of the group. She much preferred to enjoy such things from a little bit of a distance.

The children and young people paraded through the village waving Marzanna about, singing the traditional songs to welcome spring. Macaria followed behind. They stopped at each house along the way for the indulgent adults to confer their own blessings, and perhaps hand out a few sweets to the youngest children who were finally old enough to join in the annual tradition. At every puddle they passed along the way, the boys dipped the effigy down and dragged her through the muddy water as everyone clapped and laughed. As the jubilant procession gamboled along, Macaria fell further behind as her lower back hurt her more and more. Even her stomach began to tighten, aching down low. Macaria longed to go home and lie down. There would be other years to drown Marzanna with the young people of the town. As they reached the edges of the village and entered the forest, the girls at the back of the pack beckoned for her to catch up. She thought their expressions seemed frustrated, but it was hard to tell because they kept whipping around to talk to each other and flirt with the boys, full of smiles and sparkling eyes. It could have been her imagination; they could honestly want her to join them so they could enjoy each other's company. Macaria pushed herself to jog forward, pressing her lips together on a little moan. She tried to forget about the pain.

The temperature dropped as they entered the shadows of the forest and Macaria clutched her shawl a bit tighter around her. No one else seemed to notice but their cheeks did get redder and it was possible to see faint traces of their breath as they chattered like the birds of the forest. Macaria tried to distract herself by scanning the vegetation and foliage for the healing plants her mother needed, noting where she saw telltale sprouts and buds. Unfortunately, that didn't take enough of her attention to distract herself from the growing pain in her abdomen. As a hedgewitch's daughter, she'd been out in the woods identifying and collecting plants since before she could walk. Mama liked to fondly tell the stories of carrying Macaria strapped to her back when she was just an infant and how even when she was that small she would point to valuable plants and burble and giggle. Mama didn't hide her hope from her daughter that she would be a hedgewitch, too; that when the time came for Elzbieta to retire Macaria would step into her place and spend her life ministering to the people she'd grown up among. Macaria agreed it would be a fine enough life if she were ever blessed with the magical talent of a witch.

Up ahead of her, the boys found a particularly deep rut filled with spring melt and a thin scum of ice lingering on top. They hooted and hollered as they dipped and swished Marzanna with particular vigor. The girls and smaller children grabbed each other by the hands and danced in a circle around the young men. It was really more like grabbing each other's hands and running in a circle than it was like dancing, but an enterprising soul occasionally kicked out a leg as a nod to the dance. It gave Macaria a chance to catch up.

The boys pulled Marzanna up out of the rut, soaking wet with muddy water streaming down her length. It would be hard to set her on fire with her that wet. They were almost to the river and there wouldn't be much time for her to dry at all. No one but Macaria seemed to think ahead to the problems the thorough dunking would shortly cause. Macaria followed the troop with a frown, like a small cloud chasing a flock of songbirds ahead of a storm.

Sure enough, when they reached the bank of the river Marzanna refused to catch fire. Nacek kept trying to coax her sodden dress to light with the embers Aleksy brought from the forge in a lidded stone bowl. But all he managed was a sullen smolder.

"Can't we just toss her in the water?" whined Renia, the headman's daughter. "I'm starting to get chilled. Let's be done with it!"

Aleksy and Nacek frowned at her. "If we don't perform the sacrifice correctly, we could wind up with a bad growing season and a worse winter than we just had. Isn't that right, Macaria?" All eyes turned to her.

She stuttered at first, but then she found the words her mother said so many times as Macaria watched her at her spellcraft.

"Cutting corners can have disastrous consequences, especially when it comes to spellcraft," Macaria said. "We may not be witches, but this ritual will affect all of us and everyone we love. We owe it to them to get her alight."

"We've tried everything," Nacek's voice cracked and he blushed. "What should we do? Did your mother teach you anything to get wet things to burn?" Macaria shook her head and looked down at her very muddy shoes.

The lighthearted joy bled out of the crowd as everyone regarded the saturated effigy and tried to think of a way to set her alight. Macaria buried her hands deep into her apron pockets and felt ashamed that none of her power has blossomed yet, if it ever would, that she could do nothing to solve the soggy riddle of Marzanna.

"Wait!" Macaria's head came up as she whipped her hanky out of her apron pocket. It was not quite clean, but it was dry, and it would burn.

"Here," Macaria said as she scurried closer to Marzanna. "Bring it a little closer to me."

The boys obliged and Macaria twisted her hanky around the citrine necklace and slid one end through the kerchief under the effigy's chin before she tied the knot, and then tied it twice to make sure that it would not come loose.

"There," she said. "You can light the hanky and even if the rest of it doesn't catch we should be alright. The magic we can see is often just the visual symbol of the power underneath, and small things can be very powerful as long as you believe." Macaria found herself quoting her mother again.

Aleksy favored her with a broad grin as he touched the fire to the hanky. It caught easily and a cheer went up from the crowd. The boys twirled Marzanna around once more, but carefully so they didn't blow out the fitful flames on the hanky. The band of young people marched up to the edge of the riverbank and the boys lowered their arms and swung the effigy between them, once, twice, three times, and they cast her into the water.

As soon as Marzanna left their hands, the whole troop turned their backs to the water, the older children firmly pulling the younger children around despite their protests of "but why?" It was some of the darkest of bad luck to actually watch Marzanna drown. The older girls fussed over the younger children, helping them resettle shawls and jackets that had gone askew in the raucous march out to the river. Everyone resolutely kept their backs turned away from Marzanna, even Macaria. At least until she heard the hiss of the fire going out.

Without thinking she turned her head to see if Marzanna still burned, and caught sight of the effigy slowly sinking under the water. The last flames fizzled out, with the beads she'd put around Marzanna's neck floating up and looking like they would escape, except for getting caught on the bulbous stuffed head the young people made. The fire went out and the sodden wool dress dragged her down the rest of the way. Marzanna rolled a little in the water. Her face bobbed on the surface for a moment before being swallowed by the fast-moving spring melt. Macaria could have sworn the eyes drawn on the sackcloth with charcoal held her own until the very last minute when the water covered the effigy over completely. Those uneven, lopsided eyes seemed to hold a question for Macaria, but she had no answers to give them.

With a gasp Macaria whipped her head back around, her heart pounding. What had she done? She knew, perhaps better than anyone other than her mother, that she'd just doomed herself by watching Marzanna drown. Would the coming year bring her own death? Or worse still, her mother's? Macaria clutched her already aching stomach and swept the young people around her with wild eyes. No one seemed to have noticed that Macaria had broken one of the cardinal rules of drowning Marzanna. If no one saw it, did it matter? Did it even happen? Could she pretend that it didn't and will the bad luck from her with cheerful ignorance?

"Time to go," Aleksy said with a smile as he tentatively threaded his arm through Macaria's. Her heart pounded for a different reason as she let herself get lost in his eyes fringed with long, sooty lashes. She gave him a tremulous smile of her own and laid her hand on his, then they joined the rest of the party traipsing back to the village.

The older young people trod the path back at a much more sedate pace than they'd taken out to the river. Many of them took the opportunity to pair off and flirt out of sight of disapproving parents and elders. Aleksy and Macaria did not talk but snuck glances at each other with much giggling and blushing. The smaller children swirled around them like a shrieking flock of birds, chasing each other.

"Aleksy! Come play!" cried a little girl with long brown braids, tugging on his free hand. Aleksy's arm pulled from Macaria's; he laughed and stumbled before righting himself. But Macaria overbalanced and tumbled to the ground. Sharp stones dug into her hands and knees, and her forehead bounced on an exposed, gnarly root. Tears sprang to her eyes. Macaria found herself wondering if her tumble was just the first taste of bad luck.

"Macaria! Oh! I'm so sorry!" Aleksy cried as he immediately stopped cavorting and bent to help her to her feet.

"I'm fine, I'm fine," Macaria tried to keep her voice cheerful as she pushed herself to a sitting position and began to dust the forest dirt off her hands. She hissed from the pain and pulled her hands apart, staring dumbly at the scrapes and gouges that now covered her palms and the heels of her hands.

"Oh, you're in trouble now, Macaria," Renia said with a sad shake of her head. "Falling on the way back from drowning Marzanna… That truly is bad luck," she *tsk*ed.

"She only fell because I pulled her." Aleksy gave Renia a hard look and helped Macaria to her feet. "It's not her fault, she can't be blamed for it."

"Luck, good or bad, doesn't care if you deserve it or not," Renia said with a shrug.

Aleksy turned his attention back to Macaria and helped her dust the twigs and leaves from her skirts. "It's just a silly superstition about the walk back. It's not like it's part of the actual ritual. I fell two years ago on the way back and broke my wrist. Your mother set it, remember? Nothing terrible happened that year. You'll be fine." Macaria nodded and tried not to meet his eyes as she blinked tears out of her own.

"We should get back to town," Macaria murmured. "It will be dark soon and a warm supper would be good for all of us."

All the way back, the other young people and children walked with care and watched where they put their feet. No one wanted to repeat Macaria's tumble, even as Aleksy constantly reassured Macaria and everyone who would listen that everything was going to be fine and that it was just a silly superstition. He held Macaria's elbow with solicitous concern all the way to her mother's front door. Elzbieta waited for her daughter on the front step with a smug smile, until she saw the tear streaks on Macaria's cheeks.

"Oh my goodness, sweetling," Elzbieta said as she rushed forward and took Macaria from Aleksy. "What happened? Are you alright?"

The rest of the young people continued on in the dusk light, eager to get back to their own warm hearths and supper, but they still waved and called out greetings of respect to the village witch, just as well-raised boys and girls always ought to. Aleksy stayed behind to explain to Elzbieta.

"It was just a little fall," Aleksy said breathlessly. "On the way back… It's not bad luck, right?"

Elzbieta frowned. "It's no guarantee of bad luck, but it's certainly not a good start."

At the sound of her mother's words, Macaria finally burst into sobs, the fear she'd been trying to hold the whole way back spilling down her face. "I'm sorry, I'm sorry, I'm so sorry…." she sobbed. Elzbieta gathered her daughter close, petting her hair and crooning into her ear.

"Darling, darling, don't worry," she soothed. "It's probably nothing, but if it is something, we'll take care of it, yah?" Elzbieta lifted her daughter's chin and made her meet her eyes. Macaria nodded and let out a fluttery sob.

"Thank you for helping my daughter, Aleksy," Elzbieta said. "But you should head home before your parents start to worry about you."

Aleksy nodded but he still didn't move until he saw the door shut behind Macaria and Elzbieta.

Elzbieta helped Macaria to the rocking chair in front of the fire and settled a warm blanket over her shoulders.

"Now," she said crisply as she clapped her hands together. "Let's have a look at everything and once we've tended to it all I have your favorite turnip stew for supper, and then we'll tuck you into bed early. You'll be fine and fit in the morning."

Macaria nodded and held out her hands for her mother to inspect. Elzbieta nodded as she examined them with clinical detachment.

"Minor cuts and scrapes," she said. "A good cleansing and a bit of ointment and there will never be a mark once they heal. Where else?"

"Here," snuffled Macaria as she gingerly lifted the muddy hem of her skirts with her fingertips, trying to avoid brushing her tender palms, to expose her knees. Again, Elzbieta examined them closely as a healer instead of a mother.

"Superficial," she pronounced as she rose from her crouched position. "It looks like your skirts got in the way and your knees took less than your hands. We'll need to get you out of those clothes though. I need to clean those wounds and the mud doesn't help."

"I also bumped my head," Macaria sniffed as she pointed to the knot where her forehead met the tree root. Elzbieta brushed her hair away with gentle fingers and whistled through her teeth.

"That's quite a goose egg," she said. "And the scrape is deep enough to possibly leave a permanent mark. How many fingers am I holding up?"

"Two," Macaria said with a sigh. "Mama, this is silly…"

"Follow my finger with your eyes without moving your head, please," Elzbieta put a hand on Macaria's shoulder to keep her still as she passed her upraised index finger left to right and back again. "Do you know what day it is?"

"It's Wednesday and today is the day we drowned Marzanna," Macaria said as she rolled her eyes.

"Good, it doesn't seem you've scrambled your mind with the fall." Elzbieta smiled. "Is there anything else, any other pains or wounds?"

"Well," began Macaria. "My lower back and stomach have been aching."

Elzbieta frowned. "That must have been quite a fall. Come, come. We'll need to have you lie on the bed so I can get a good look at your back and belly."

"It started before the fall, before we went out into the woods, really," Macaria said as she stood, and then she gasped as her whole lower body clenched and she felt wetness between her thighs.

"Aaiiee! Something is wrong. I must have broken something inside," Macaria cried as she nearly doubled over from the pain.

"Let me see," Elzbieta said with a tight voice as she flipped up her daughter's skirts to search for the wound. And then she began to laugh.

"Mother! How can you laugh at me at a time like this?" Macaria frowned and slapped her mother's hands away from her skirts, taking a hobbling step away. "I need your best spells, not to be ridiculed."

"Oh, sweetling," Elzbieta said with a smile as she put her hands to her cheeks. "You're in no danger of bleeding to death. Your moon time has finally come upon you, girl. It's the blood of your womanhood, not an accident."

Macaria's face blanched. "You mean this is what it's going to feel like every month?"

Elzbieta took her daughter's arm and guided her over to the corner where they kept their tin washtub. "You get used to it after a time," she said with a shrug. "Come now, let's get you cleaned up and I'll explain a few things while you wash."

Elzbieta settled Macaria into her own bed on the main floor with every pillow in the house piled behind her so she could sit up comfortably. Elzbieta would sleep up in the loft that night to spare Macaria climbing up and down the ladder. Elzbieta fed her some white willow bark tea and then presented her daughter with a bowl of her favorite turnip stew.

"Isn't there some spell you can cast that makes the pain go away?" Macaria pleaded as she stirred her stew.

"A witches' moon blood is not something to be trifled with, child," Elzbieta soothed. "There is power in it, and until we understand your power and your cycle, the less intervention the better." Macaria leaned into her mother's hand she smoothed the damp strands of hair from her forehead.

"But we don't even know if I really am a witch," Macaria said with a heavy sigh.

Elzbieta smiled. "I believe your power will show itself soon. The time around the first moon blood is a common time for young witches to bloom. But here, let me try something."

Elzbieta clucked her tongue and made kissing noises at one of the half dozen cats they shared their home with. A slender brown tabby female answered her call. Elzbieta picked her up and cooed and petted and scratched her until the cat purred noisily. With gentle hands, Elzbieta laid the cat on Macaria's abdomen and took her empty stew bowl from her.

"Keep petting her so she'll stay," Elzbieta instructed. "How does that feel?"

"Her heat, it really helps," Macaria murmured with surprise as she continued to scratch the cat behind her ears and stroke her.

"Indeed," Elzbieta said with a wink. "Cats are good for more than just spell work and vermin control. You see why so many good wives keep a few around the house?"

"Mm-Hmm..." Macaria agreed as she drowsed, finally warm and comfortable with the white willow bark tea and the purring cat working their miraculous ways on her womanly aches.

Elzbieta leaned over and kissed her sleepy daughter on the forehead. "Sleep, my love. We can talk more in the morning."

Chapter Two

The light of dawn illuminated the first clue that Macaria's power had indeed begun to manifest, but not in a way that Macaria or Elzbieta expected or wanted.

"Mama! Mama!" Macaria cried.

Elzbieta scrambled down the ladder, rubbing the sleep from her eyes. "Did you overflow your rags? It's not the end of the world, girl, everything can be washed."

"No," Macaria moaned. "The cat... She... She..."

"Sometimes they get bored and leave in the night, Macaria," Elzbieta sighed. "You know as well as I do that you can't make a cat do what a cat doesn't want to do. Maybe one of the others will..."

Elzbieta stopped at the edge of the bed, her words dried up in an instant. Macaria sat up straight with her hands over her mouth and tears streaming down her cheeks, and a dead cat draped over her belly. The cat had been dead long enough to be cold.

"I didn't do anything, I swear," Macaria babbled. "She was alive when I fell asleep and when I woke she was cold..."

"Hush, child." Elzbieta held up a hand and Macaria obeyed immediately. "This could be nothing more than happenstance.

Perhaps she was older than we realized and it was just her time. Remember, we didn't have this one from a kitten."

"But what if it's not happenstance?" Macaria groaned. "Mama, I didn't tell you everything about yesterday. I left one part out."

Elzbieta sucked in her breath and raised her chin. "You know better than to keep secrets from me, girl. What happened? Tell me now, all of it." Her voice was sharp.

Macaria's tears flowed harder and she covered her face with her hands, but she didn't hide a single detail from her mother as she sobbed and stuttered her way through a full explanation from the moment she'd left her mother's cottage to join the ritual to when she'd arrived back, muddy and scraped. She included it all—how she considered keeping the citrine beads, how they couldn't get Marzanna to light, and how she watched Marzanna as she sank under the water and felt as if the eyes drawn with charcoal knew something, and through the fall on the way back that she thought maybe was the first sign of the awful luck she was sure to be cursed with.

Elzbieta went pale as she lowered herself to the stool she'd left next to her daughter's bed the night before. "It could all still just be happenstance, Macaria. There are things we don't tell people not initiated into the mysteries about the rituals we allow them."

"Like what?" Macaria lowered her hands from her eyes and rubbed the back of her hand across her nose.

"Seeing Marzanna drown is not a death sentence, but it can have some dark meanings." Elzbieta spoke softly as her eyes stared off into the empty distance.

"Like what? Mama, you're scaring me," Macaria's voice trembled and she hugged her shoulders.

Elzbieta came back to herself, shaking her head as if clearing a fog. "I cannot say anything yet. I need to look at a few things. I don't want to frighten you unless I have no choice." Elzbieta stood and hurried to her workbench.

"You're frightening me already, Mama." Macaria wept harder. "What is going on?"

Elzbieta returned to her daughter's bedside drawing on thick leather gloves, just like the kind the local blacksmith wore but sized for her more delicate hands.

"The fright you have now is nothing compared to what it could be, based on what I find," Elzbieta said. She carefully lifted the dead cat away from Macaria, not letting any of her skin touch the skin of her daughter. "Just wait there quietly and don't touch anything. As soon as I have something of use to tell you, I will." Macaria watched her mother carry the cat outside, as she twisted her fingers together.

Elzbieta came back half an hour later with a grim look on her face and her silver athame bloody in her fist, her leather gloves smeared with more blood.

Macaria gasped, pressing her fingers to her lips. "What is it, Mama?"

"Hush, child," Elzbieta nearly growled as she made for her workbench slid the blade into the waiting basin of sacred salt-water. She stripped off her gloves and tossed them into the fire, then grabbed her deck of tarot cards.

She laid the thick stack of cards on a flat spot at the foot of Macaria's bed and took a step back. "Shuffle and cut," she said in a tight, clipped voice. Macaria picked up the cards, turning the familiar corners in her hands, thinking of her question so the cards would respond to her energy.

Macaria's hands worked the motions of shuffling and cutting the cards without a thought, her fingers long used to the motions from the many times she'd played with them as a child or begged her mother to read her cards as she got older. She kneeled on the bed and watched her mother's face. Macaria saw nothing there beyond her mother's grim expression. She laid out the two roughly even stacks full of her energy and her questions, then sat back on her heels.

Her mother picked up the stack closest to her and flipped the top three cards — Death, Death, Death. She let that stack drop from nerveless fingers and they scattered on the floor, every face that showed was Death. She snatched up the second stack and flipped

the top three cards—Death, Death, Death. Elzbieta threw them away from her with a howl and dropped to her knees, collapsing in on herself and sobbing into her hands.

"Mama? Mother? What is it?" Macaria's voice trembled.

Elzbieta's shoulders worked up and down. Macaria held her breath as she waited for her mother to speak. When Elzbieta finally spoke, she choked out the words in a thin, trembling voice.

"Your power is upon you; you are of the Sisterhood of Witches. And the power that has settled into your bones is a rare and potent one. You know as well as I do that there is only one card for Death in a deck. Yet every card I turn for you is Death. You are a death witch."

"No, no, no," Macaria moaned. "This can't be possible. Do it again. Show me the cards again!"

In silence, Elzbieta crawled around on the floor gathering the scattered cards, tears dripping off her nose and chin. When she had them all she handed them to Macaria careful to not let their fingers touch, her eyes full of sadness. She shuffled and cut them again, laying both stacks on the end of the bed as before. Elzbieta picked up one stack and nodded to the other.

"You turn them this time," she said in a trembling voice.

Macaria turned the cards herself this time—Death, Death, Death.

"Someone has fouled your deck and cursed it," Macaria sobbed as she dashed the cards away with a swipe of her hand. The cards fluttered to the floor. Death peered from every one that landed face up.

Silently, Elzbieta turned the top three cards from the stack in her hands onto the stool next to the bed—The Hanged Man, The Sun, Judgment.

Without a word she set the remaining cards on Macaria's bed again and tapped the stack with the tip of her finger.

Macaria drew the top three cards once again, her hand shaking so hard she dropped them as soon as she took them—Death, Death, Death. Macaria wailed and held out her arms to her mother.

Elzbieta burst into fresh tears and clutched her arms around her middle. "Oh my child, my dearest…" she sobbed. "You don't know how much I want to hold you right now. But if I touch you before you gain control of your power, I will suffer the same fate as the cat."

Macaria lowered her empty arms in front of her and started keening. Her head bowed down, the curtain of her thick brown hair covering her face as sobs wracked her shoulders. Elzbieta dropped to the floor and wept too.

After what seemed like forever, both of their tears slowed and the sobs turned to fitful hiccups.

"What do we do now?" Macaria whispered.

"I cannot teach you as I had always planned to do," Elzbieta said, her voice rough from grief. "You will need to tutor under a death witch until you master your power. Another death witch is the only person who can safely touch you until you do."

"And then what? Do I come back here to learn herbcraft from you so I can take your place as we had always planned?" Macaria asked.

"No." Elzbieta's voice cracked. "After you have mastered yourself and your teacher is satisfied that your training is done, you will go to the Polish Council of Witches. They will tell you what they need you to do. You will become a rare and valuable tool for our community. You must take care to not be used as a pawn in political games."

Macaria clutched her stomach and shook her head from side to side. "No, no, no… I can't do that. Please don't make me do that, Mama."

"I have less choice in this matter than you do, child," Elzbieta said as she blew her nose into a handkerchief.

"How can you have less choice? You're telling me the Council might turn me into some sort of a tool for their own purposes."

"And you will have the power of death in your hands, Macaria." Elzbieta fixed her daughter with serious eyes. "The only way you become a pawn is if you allow yourself to be one. If you pay attention to those who try to trick you and stay to the moral code I raised you by, no one can use you against your will. Your hands will always be clean."

"Hands that deal death can never be clean," Macaria whispered with a shudder.

Elzbieta shook her head as she picked herself up off the floor. "You have much to learn, child. I cannot teach you as much as you will need to know but I can teach you this—Death is not evil, sometimes death is even a blessing."

"How…" Macaria started but her mother held up her hand for silence.

"Your teacher will give you the knowledge and tools you will need," she said in a forlorn murmur. "I don't want to explain something critical incorrectly and corrupt anything she might teach you."

"So, what now?" Macaria asked as she scrubbed her eyes with the heels of her hands.

"Now, we send word to the Council that a new death witch is born, then we wait." Elzbieta crossed the room back to her workbench again and threw open the window above it. She cawed out the rough call of the crow in short, sharp bursts.

Moments later a large crow landed in her windowsill, then hopped down onto her workbench. Elzbieta smiled down fondly at the bird, caressing his head as she pulled a few small beans out of her apron pocket for him to eat. Elzbieta sighed as she watched him gobble them down.

"I never thought this would be a message I'd have to give you to carry," she murmured.

When the crow finished his beans, he bobbed his head to Elzbieta, leaning in toward her. She laid her cheek against the top of his head, closing her eyes. She whispered words that Macaria could not hear, no matter how hard she strained. When Elzbieta was done, she lifted her head the crow hopped back once. He cocked his head to the side and cawed.

"Yes, I'm sure," Elzbieta said with her head bowed.

The crow looked across the room at Macaria and back to Elzbieta again. Macaria could have almost sworn the crow sighed before he cawed one last time and then hopped back up onto the windowsill. With a great flap of his wings, he took to the air. Macaria stayed quiet as she watched her mother's back, rigid with apprehension, until the bird disappeared from the sky.

When the knock came at the door early the next morning, Elzbieta and Macaria both jumped. They sat at the table eating their breakfast porridge across from each other instead of side by side, as had been their custom since Macaria was small. They exchanged surprised looks and raised eyebrows. Then the knock came again, more impatient this time.

Elzbieta rose and brushed her hands down the front of her apron, prepared to send the visitor away. But when she opened the door she saw that this visitor would not be denied. She stepped back out of the way, bowing low, sweeping her arm out to encompass her whole home.

"I did not expect you this soon, Sister," she said. "Please, be welcome."

In strode a slender woman dressed all in black, wrapped in a thick, wool winter cape and black leather gloves despite the thaw and rising temperatures. Her skin was bone pale and she had watery gray eyes deep-set over high, sharp cheekbones. She'd swept her ebony hair back in a tight chignon at the nape of her neck. The crow sent with Elzbieta's message to the Council perched on her right shoulder. She fixed cool eyes on Macaria, seeming to take her full measure in a single glance. Elzbieta closed the door behind her, all the blood drained from her face. Macaria swallowed hard and felt the porridge turn to stone in her belly. This was obviously the death witch her mother requested.

"Your messenger saw me on the road and stopped to deliver the news before he flew on," the death witch said, her voice a mere dusty whisper that crept into every corner of Macaria's ear.

"I sent my own bird on to inform the Council I am taking your daughter as my new apprentice."

Elzbieta's crow fluttered and hopped to the workbench from the death witch's shoulder, where he tilted his head and let out a short questioning croak. Without taking her eyes from the death witch, Elzbieta absently pulled a few beans from her apron pocket and laid them on the bench, then opened the window so he could take his leave when he wished.

"Doesn't the Council usually assign apprentices outside of bloodlines?" Elzbieta tried to keep her voice from trembling and only partially succeeded.

The death witch took her eyes from Macaria for the first time since entering the room. She looked Elzbieta up and down. "Not for our specialty, we handle our apprentice assignments ourselves."

She returned her gaze to Macaria, then crossed the room to her. She took hold of Macaria's chin, turning her face left and right.

"So," she said in the same cool whisper. "Your power came on with your moon time, yes?"

"Y-y-y-yes," Macaria stuttered.

The death witch's face relaxed and some warmth crept into her pale cheeks. "There is no need to fear me, child. I am here to guide you." She sighed and tilted her head to the side. "But I do understand your fear. It was not so long ago that I was in your place, faced with a great and terrible mystery while my body decided to change on me."

"Is it common for death witches to get their power with their moon times?" Macaria asked her voice trembling.

"No, it is actually very uncommon. It is a sign of particularly strong power in a death witch," she replied. "Which is why I am to take you on as an apprentice rather than one of the others of our specialty. I am the only one who might be able to handle you."

Macaria blanched. "Might?"

"Well, probably." The death witch gave her a sly smile.

"Can I offer you some breakfast?" Elzbieta broke in. "We have porridge and tea."

"Just some tea, thank you. We can't tarry long." She turned her gaze back to her apprentice. "I was on my way to an important task when your mother's bird found me. I think it would be good for you to see our work in action before I start your instruction, apprentice."

"Yes, ma'am," Macaria murmured as she bobbed her head.

"Mmmm… Good manners, this is an auspicious start." The death witch smiled and nodded toward Macaria's half-empty porridge bowl. "Finish your breakfast and then pack your things quickly, only what you can carry yourself in a small bag. We are on a schedule."

Macaria rose from the table and bobbed a curtsy to her new teacher. "I don't think I can eat any more, ma'am. I'll just go pack. I don't want to hold us back."

The death witch eased herself into the seat Macaria just vacated as she watched the girl scurry off with her eyes downcast. Elzbieta set a fresh mug of steaming tea in front of her.

"Sugar?"

The death witch shook her head and slipped her hands out of her supple black calfskin gloves to wrap her pale, slender fingers around the cup. "I am on the road regularly and must often do without some of the more lovely things in life. Best not to remind myself how much I love them…" She favored Elzbieta with a small smile.

Elzbieta glanced up to the open loft where Macaria was packing, then back to the death witch. "I am uncertain of the dictates here, but am I allowed to know the name of the woman who is taking my daughter on her dark journey?"

The death witch's smile turned rueful as she tilted her head to the side. "You really have been steeped in a lot of the old stories, haven't you?"

Elzbieta blushed and stared at the floor.

"I am Joanna Lewandowski, Koniec of the Polish Council of Witches, and your daughter will eventually be free to visit you when she can between assignments. She just cannot follow in your footsteps; she has a different path."

Elzbieta nodded and dashed tears from her eyes.

"Really," Joanna reached out and laid her hand on Elzbieta's. Elzbieta stifled a gasp and froze. "It's not a death sentence, and there is good to be done with the power. You will see."

Macaria presented herself, changed into her plainest and sturdiest clothes for traveling, with a leather satchel slung across her body. She said nothing and stood with her head bowed and her hands clasped in front of her.

Elzbieta reached to straighten her daughter's collar but stopped herself just in time. "You remembered everything? Even all your moon supplies?"

"Yes, Mama," Macaria whispered as she blushed and ground her toe into the floorboard.

"Then it is time for us to go," Joanna said crisply as she stood and slid her gloves back on, muffling the sound as she clapped her hands together. She walked to the door, leaving behind the untouched mug of tea.

Macaria lifted her head. She murmured, "Goodbye, Mama," wiped the tears from her eyes, and turned to follow her teacher.

"Goodbye, sweetling." Elzbieta's voice sounded lost and empty.

Macaria paused on the threshold. "When I come back I'll kiss you twice, Mama, once for this goodbye and once for hello."

And then she was gone.

Chapter Three

Joanna and Macaria walked in silence from the cottage and into the woods, continuing for some time before Joanna sighed.

"We're not going to get very far if you won't even speak to me," she said, giving Macaria a sidelong look.

Macaria pressed her lips together and stared hard at the ground as she trudged along. Joanna waited for a moment and was rewarded when Macaria took a shaky breath and began to talk.

"I thought students were supposed to be silent and only speak when spoken to," she said.

"Would that be the way your mother would have taught you, had you followed her into the ways of the hedgewitch?" Joanna asked.

"No, she's my mother, we know each other," the words tumbled out of Macaria. "All the other masters I've seen treat their apprentices a certain way. I thought I was supposed to be quiet and listen to your wisdom…" Macaria trailed off and dared a sidelong look at Joanna herself. Joanna was smiling.

"Have you ever seen another witch teacher-apprentice pairing?" Joanna asked.

Macaria frowned. "Well, no. The only other witches I've met besides Mama have been some of her friends when they came to visit. And once there was a traveling witch, all the way from Italy! She was delivering a copy of some important prophecy to the Council." Macaria's eyes grew bright and she turned to look Joanna full in the face, a slight spring infecting her step. Joanna stifled a giggle.

"Oh, my girl," she said. "I think we're going to be just fine." She stopped and laid a hand on Macaria's shoulder. "A witch teacher-apprentice pairing is supposed to be more like what you would have had with your mother rather than what you see with other professions. Magic work, especially our kind of magic work, touches on deep emotions and power; we need to have an unshakeable bond and be able to trust each other."

Macaria nodded hard, her eyes wide.

"Now," Joanna said. "There will be times that I ask for your silence, but that is not for you to prove your obedience to me. It is so you don't say the wrong thing at the wrong time and foul a spell before you know better. Understand?"

"Yes, ma'am."

"Good," Joanna patted Macaria on the shoulder and started off again in long, fast strides, Macaria trotting in her wake. "I will ask you to be silent and just watch when we get where we are going, but for right now I want to hear about you. I would like to know about my new student."

"Ma'am?" Macaria puffed as she tried to keep up.

"Tell me about yourself, you silly featherhead," Joanna said with a chuckle and a shake of her head, but she did slow her stride. "Let's start with your name, for example."

"Macaria, my name is Macaria," she said as she blushed.

Joanna stopped dead in her tracks to stare at Macaria. Macaria almost tripped over her.

"What?" Macaria asked.

"Your mother is surprised you turned out to be a death witch when she named you after a minor Greek death deity?" Joanna's voice was incredulous.

Macaria blushed. "Mama said she heard the name whispered in her dreams when she was pregnant with me. She thought it was pretty."

Joanna shook her head as she started off again, this time at a more reasonable pace.

"I think we are going to have an interesting time, you and I," she said as she led the way down a narrower path to take them in a southerly direction. "Let's go back to the part where you tell me about yourself, Macaria."

They continued their trek through the woods accompanied by the sound of small bird song and Macaria's chatter.

Their journey ended in the midafternoon at another cottage tucked along the edge of the Polish wilderness, looking out over an expansive meadow full of tall grass and wildflowers. Joanna stopped on the rise overlooking the trim little cottage. A thin tendril of smoke curled up out of its chimney.

"Alright then," Joanna said with a heavy sigh. "You are about to witness one of the kinder duties of our work, but it will likely be difficult for you."

"What is it?" Macaria looked serious.

"I am to bring death to a very sick man," Joanna said in a soft, husky whisper. "He is in much pain and his affairs are in order; he has said all of his good-byes. He was of service to the Council when he was young, so the Council sent me to grant him comfort in his hour of need."

Macaria's jaw dropped. "You're going to kill a man and that is supposed to be a kinder duty?"

Joanna frowned and gave her a harsh look. "Haven't you listened to a word I've said? He is in pain, hideous pain, and he has no tasks left to him in this world. Yes, this is a kinder duty, to release one from pain and misery when there is no reason to continue."

Macaria swallowed hard and shrank under her teacher's glare. "Does he want this? Does he really want to die?" she squeaked.

"If he did not want to die and he was not ready, he would not have sent word to the Council begging them to send a death witch," Joanna snapped.

Macaria cringed and whispered, "I'm sorry. I won't question you again."

Joanna sighed and pinched the bridge of her nose, shutting her eyes.

"I want you to question me, girl," she said. "Our work is full of many gray areas. Dealing with the forces we must deal with makes it easy to fall into the darker regions of magic. But this, *this* is not one of those gray areas. This is well and truly the kindest thing we can do with our gift."

Macaria nodded hard and pressed her lips together.

"There is so much I need to undo in your head before I can really begin to teach you, Macaria. Death is not evil. Death is a threshold, a passage. Yes, it leaves those behind in grief and pain, but it is not because of death that people grieve and hurt, that comes because of love. When you love a person and you lose them it hurts. It's supposed to hurt. How can you truly know the sweetness of love without the bitterness of loss?"

"I…" Macaria started.

"If a person dies and leaves behind no pain in the people around them, then that is truly a sorrowful thing. There was no love, and a life without love…" Joanna gave a shuddering sigh and turned her head away, silent for a moment.

"Listen to me now, girl," Joanna said as she straightened her shoulders, lifting her chin and casting her eyes forward. "Once we get to the cottage, you will stand where I tell you to stand and you will not make a sound. You will speak to no one. You will touch no one. If I give you any instruction you will obey me without question. Have I made myself clear?"

"Yes, ma'am," Macaria murmured and bobbed a curtsey.

Joanna raised an eyebrow. "It's likely they will not invite us to stay once I am done. Most people don't want to invite the witch who just took their loved one from them for tea and cakes." She looked Macaria up and down once and nodded at what she saw, then headed down the rise without another word.

The soon-to-be widow, with bloodshot eyes and a well-worn hanky at her nose, responded to Joanna's gentle knock. She tried to hide her cringe with a nod and a bow, but it was clear she feared the woman on her doorstep. She scuttled back and opened the door wide to avoid any chance of her skirts brushing those of a death witch. She bowed low and her shoulders hitched with silent sobs as she gestured without a sound for Joanna and Macaria to enter.

The snug, one-room cottage with an open loft was very like the one Macaria had left behind. There was the hearth and eating area toward her left that didn't have clear boundaries between it and where the woman of the house plied her work. Macaria spotted a small back strap loom and spinning wheel, and the other accoutrements of fiber craft. On the opposite side of the hearth were the sleeping areas, the large bed for the matriarch and patriarch, and a loft up above for older children or servants.

As she scanned over the familiar layout of the living space, Macaria noticed the pervasive stench of deep sickness. Despite the open windows and curtains blowing in the breeze, the surfaces so clean they almost glowed, and beeswax candles standing lit on almost every flat surface in the cottage, Macaria almost gagged and started to bring her hand up to her nose. Joanna shot her a sideways gaze so cold Macaria's hand froze, then dropped limply to her side. She resolved to breathe through her mouth for the duration and hoped that whatever spell Joanna needed to perform was a quick one.

A young man stood up from the bench and broad table by the hearth, his eyes just as bloodshot as the woman who answered the door.

"Are you sure this is necessary?" he asked, his voice trembling.

Joanna inclined her head to him and gave him a gentle smile. "I am sure this was requested, and I am sure this is a kindness."

As the woman sobbed into her handkerchief, the young man reached out to pat her on the shoulder. Joanna paused for a moment before she spoke again.

"I have come to ease Jakub's pain and leave you both to your grief," Joanna said.

"How dare you be so familiar?" the woman hissed as her handkerchief fell from hands suddenly bent to claws.

"Agata!" rose a weak and querulous voice from amid the thick pile of blankets and pillows on the bed. "Stop harassing the poor witch and let her come to me. I asked for this. Abide by my wishes, woman!" Jakub's last words were lost in a flurry of coughing and choking.

Joanna drifted toward the bed like smoke, the barest twitch of her hand at her side bade Macaria follow her. She stopped at the edge of the bed and smiled down on the frail figure bundled there. She gave a spot close behind her a quick but firm glance. Macaria took her place to watch her teacher demonstrate her first death spell.

A near-skeletal hand rose from the blankets, the skin nearly pale as bone itself. Joanna gently clasped it.

"Ah, I thought you would give me my grace straight away, and yet I still breathe," Jakub croaked.

"You know I have a protocol, you old goat," Joanna said fondly.

"Between friends, we must have protocol?" Jakub's voice came in a sad whisper.

Joanna reached out with her free hand and wiped a tear from Jakub's cheek. "With death, we must, even if we broke all the rules in life."

Agata's face drew down in an angry glower, but after Jakub's last rebuke she did not let another word cross her lips. The young man standing next to her crossed his arms over his chest and frowned. But he likewise said nothing.

Joanna stroked a few fine strands away from Jakub's forehead and leaned close over him, his one hand still firmly clasped in her own.

"Is it your desire, come to with careful thought and consideration, to leave your earthly bonds?" Joanna's voice did not rise above a whisper yet somehow each word rang clearly in the ears of every person in the room. Macaria held back a gasp as she saw the air swirl near Jakub's head. She longed to rub her eyes but she dared not disturb the ritual.

"It is," Jakub wheezed from his bed.

"Have you set all your affairs in order and said all of your farewells?" Joanna asked the second question.

"I have," Jakub whispered, and then fell into another coughing fit. Macaria could hear the breath crackle in and out of his lungs from where she stood. "Dammit, woman, I know you can make it quicker than this." Jakub groaned.

This time Macaria was sure she saw something flutter past Jakub's mouth as he spoke. She stole a glance at Jakub's family. They seemed upset, of course, but gave no sign they saw the fluttering.

"Only one more question, dear," Joanna breathed, her brow knitted with sorrow. She paused a moment and cleared her throat. "Will you hold the Polish Witches Council innocent of your death and bind all your kin from holding them liable?"

"Yes, yes," Jakub cried out with as much strength as he could muster. "Please," he begged. "Make the pain stop. Agata kept making me wait, hoping some medicine or charm would let me live. I just want the pain to stop."

"Rest." The word came out on the barest whisper of Joanna's breath as she leaned forward and laid a gentle kiss on Jakub's forehead.

One last breath sighed out of his lungs. And then he was gone.

Macaria clamped her jaw tight so that she didn't cry out. She saw them clearly this time. Tiny Fae, no larger than her hand, flew and dipped about Jakub like bats after insects in the night. Their skin was gray, their hair was black, and their wings… their wings resembled bat wings, but they were painted in the violets and indigos of late evening. Macaria looked at Joanna but Joanna gave no indication that there was anything unusual happening at all.

They all stood in silence, listening to the breeze murmur outside, watching the unmoving figure of Jakub. Joanna still held his hand and gazed upon him tenderly.

"Get out," Agata growled, breaking the spell of the silence. "You've done what you came here to do. You've rubbed it in my face that there was a part of my Jakub that always belonged to you. Now, get out!" She spat the words as if they were poison and jabbed her finger at the door.

Joanna nodded to Agata, but with unhurried grace she straightened Jakub's limbs into dignified repose. She turned to Agata and the young man and dropped an elegant curtsy with her head bowed and her eyes downcast. Macaria hurried to imitate her teacher but was far less polished.

Joanna recited the ritual words, "May peace and serenity enter this house. May your hearts be at ease that Jakub has found his release."

Agata spat. "Just get out, you foul harlot."

Joanna nodded again, her face smooth and untroubled despite the anger and insults Agata flung. She turned to the door and gestured for Macaria to go before her. Macaria opened the door and found herself bowing to Joanna as she crossed the threshold with an unhurried pace and her head held high. As Macaria closed the door behind her, she saw Agata collapse into the arms of the young man and weep into his chest. She turned to find Joanna already halfway across the meadow, making for the forest. She hurried after her.

"What was that all about?" Macaria huffed as she caught up.

Joanna held up her hand for silence but did not turn her head or break her pace.

"There are some things you may not know about me yet, child." Her voice came out in a rough croak. "Attend to your lessons, work hard, and earn my trust, and you may yet hear the story that led to what happened just now."

"But the F-f-fae," Macaria stuttered. "I've never seen Fae like that before. What were they?"

Joanna paused. Her head snapped around to Macaria. "You can see them already?"

Macaria gulped. "Small Fae, like pixies, but dark colors instead of bright ones. Flying around Jakub's head like bats as you performed the ritual."

"You shouldn't be able to see them yet..." Joanna's voice trailed off. She started walking again. Macaria hurried after her.

"See what yet?"

"Nyxies. They usually don't show themselves until much later in your training." Joanna's voice trembled. She worked her jaw, trying to hold in a sob.

"What are..." Macaria began.

"Not now, Macaria! Please!" Joanna stopped and took a deep quivering breath. "I will answer all of your questions, but now is not the time."

Macaria couldn't have sworn to it, but she thought she saw a single tear creep down Joanna's cheek.

She held her tongue.

Chapter four

Joanna set a hard pace for the rest of the afternoon and spoke little. When she finally paused, she let out a deep sigh and closed her eyes as her shoulders sagged. After a moment, she raised her head and said, "Gather some wood, child. We need a fire."

Macaria made quick work of the wood gathering and made it back to the small clearing where they had stopped, but Joanna was nowhere to be seen. Macaria set down her armload of wood and turned to look for any sign of where her mistress had gone. She saw nothing. With a sigh, she cleared their camp and built up the fire. It crackled cheerily by the time Joanna stepped into the ring of firelight holding two dead rabbits by their hind legs. Macaria began to dig in her bag for her knife to skin them. Her stomach already growled and she didn't want to waste another moment getting the plump rabbits on the fire.

"Before dinner preparations," Joanna said. "You must practice your skills."

Macaria's mouth hung open. "What skills?"

"Your skills in manipulating death," Joanna said as she squatted down next to Macaria and laid the rabbits on the ground between them.

"But... But..." Macaria sputtered. "I only found out what I am this morning. I have no skills yet."

"You must start learning sometime," Joanna said with a gentle smile. "Which one do you prefer?" She gestured to the rabbits.

"Well, I'm hungry so I'd like to have the bigger one, but you're my teacher so manners say I offer to take the poorer meal for myself," Macaria said with a frown.

"The bigger one then," Joanna said, moving the smaller gray rabbit to the side and leaving the stout brown rabbit between them. "I took both of them with the death touch," Joanna continued. "And now I will wake this one and then you will take it again with your touch."

Macaria looked from the rabbit to her teacher and back again several times with her mouth gaping even wider.

"You're going to bring it back to life? I thought we were death witches," Macaria said. "We give death with a touch, not life."

"We are death witches, but our power is to bring death *or* send it away with our touch."

"So, if a huntsman shot my dog," Macaria began with a thoughtful tilt of her head. "I could bring the dog back?"

Joanna shook her head. "And then the poor hound would die again just as painfully as the first time. We can bring the life back, but a wounded person or animal will still bleed out."

Macaria frowned. "Can we bring back someone who has been dead a long time? Assuming they won't just bleed to death again?"

"There are... problems... with that scenario." Joanna pursed her lips and focused down on the ground. "The longer a spirit is away from a body the harder it is to bring it back, if it can come back at all. And then there is the practical problem of the decay of the flesh. One unscrupulous, and some say mad, witch brought back the long-dead... It did not go well. In the end, we had to curb her. We lost many of our own bringing her down."

Macaria's eyes grew wide. "What was her name? Why have I never heard of her?"

"Tonight's lesson is a lesson in practical matters, not history," Joanna said, her voice hard at first but then she softened. "We do not speak of her because we don't want to frighten people more than we already do, and we don't want anyone else to attempt what she did. Someday, if you prove that you have a good head on your shoulders, I will tell you her story and give you her name. If you prove that you can be trusted with that knowledge, someday you may know how she did what she did. But that time is not tonight. Tonight, we deal with the rabbit." She gestured to the unmoving creature between them.

"But I killed the cat by accident! While I was asleep!" Macaria protested. "I have no idea how I did it."

"Did you know how to identify herbs on your own before your mother showed you how?" Joanna asked.

"Of course not," Macaria said. "No one knows everything right off. One must be taught."

"Exactly. I am not going to ask you to do anything without proper guidance, but it is imperative that we get some measure of control over your power. We must minimize unintentional deaths."

"Minimize?" Macaria asked. She swallowed hard.

"Yes, child," Joanna said with a not unkind smile. "You've already taken one life without meaning to. Fortunately, it was only a cat and not your mother or one of the boys in the village as you indulged in a kiss."

Macaria's face flamed as she looked everywhere but at Joanna.

Joanna's expression grew severe. "There will be more unintentional death before your training is through. If you get excited or distracted, you will lose your grip on your power. That is why your first two lessons are learning to control the touch with concentration, and then learning how to bring the living back when you inevitably fail."

Macaria's face blanched. "I don't want this," she whispered without thinking.

Joanna drew the plump brown rabbit into her lap and stroked its still, cold fur. "I don't think there has been a single one of us who *wanted* this, especially in the beginning. We death witches are a smaller sisterhood within the Sisterhood of Witches. There are nine of us here in Poland, maybe another two dozen throughout the rest of Europe. The Witches in the United Kingdom have half a dozen at most. They may have fewer. They are very closed-mouthed about such things."

"But most of us," Joanna continued. "By the end of our training, we come to a certain peace. We come to see the necessity, and sometimes even the beauty in what we do."

"Beauty in death?" Macaria's voice was incredulous.

Joanna smiled softly, her eyes focused somewhere far away as she continued to stroke the rabbit. "Was there not beauty in releasing Jakob from the pain of his earthly bonds? The illness that consumed him would have continued, painfully, for quite some time without my intervention. Was there not kindness and grace in allowing him to end his suffering at a time of his own choosing?" She raised her gaze to meet Macaria's eyes.

"I... I... well..." Macaria stuttered and blushed. "I suppose..."

"The answer is *yes*, my student," Joanna said in a voice that brooked no argument. "Preventing pain and allowing people some control in lives where they often have so little is good. People may fear us, Macaria, but they need us and the good we can do. Once you come to this conclusion, you will stop wishing you were never blessed with such a dark gift."

"And what if I never come to the conclusion that this 'gift' is good? What if I never see the beauty and kindness in death? What if I still wish I didn't have this power even after I know how to use it?" The words and the fear that came with them poured out of Macaria like a river.

"Then I will teach you how to use your power upon yourself, and you will give your own self the final blessing," Joanna said in a soft voice with grief in her eyes.

"How many?" Macaria asked in a whisper.

Joanna shrugged. "Half? Two-thirds? Not every witch born with the death touch has the fortitude to handle it."

Macaria's eyes went wide. "Have you had apprentices before me who did not have the fortitude?"

"I am young as death witches go," Joanna said with a sigh. "If you complete your training and have the courage to enter the sisterhood, to live with this gift, you will be my first."

"But you didn't..." Macaria began.

"Now, to start your lesson," Joanna interrupted her. "In a moment, I will bring this rabbit back to life. You will practice how to reign in or unleash your death touch on command. It will likely take you several attempts to get it right. Please try to keep your emotions under control. The more upset you get, the more difficult it will be."

"I'm not ready!" Macaria protested.

"That doesn't matter," Joanna said as she ran her hand down the rabbit's back again until it shivered back to life. Immediately, it tried to leap from Joanna's lap. But her grip was strong, and she held it fast. It struggled for a few more moments, then subsided into terrified trembling.

"Now, what I want you to do," Joanna instructed. "Is to close your eyes and clear your mind as much as you can. I want you to reach out and touch the rabbit, but please be careful not to touch me. I do have defenses, but I might lose hold of half of our dinner." She smiled at Macaria, obviously trying to put her at ease. "I want you to pay attention to what you feel as you touch the rabbit. What pulls and pushes in your mind? What sensations do you feel on your skin, in your heart?"

Macaria swallowed hard and nodded. "Then what?"

"After the rabbit dies by your touch," Joanna said matter-of-factly. "I will bring it back again, and we will repeat the exercise until you can touch the rabbit without killing it."

"How long will that take?" Macaria asked with a frown. "I'm starving."

"It takes as long as it takes. If you are so hungry, I suggest you learn quickly."

Macaria grimaced but she reached forward with a quivering hand to touch the rabbit. Her fingertips barely touched its fur and the rabbit shuddered and died again.

"What did you feel?"

"Horrified," Macaria said as a shiver rolled down her spine.

Joanna sighed. "No girl, what did you feel in your mind, your heart, your soul?"

Macaria blinked. "I don't know."

"Pay closer attention this time," Joanna ordered with a frown. "Now, do it again." She stroked the rabbit's back and it twitched back to life. Again, it tried to escape. Again, Joanna held it fast, her eyes locked on Macaria.

Macaria squared her shoulders and reached for the rabbit once more. She sank her fingertips deep into its fur and even though the rabbit fell lifeless, she held her hand there for several beats of her own heart, eyes closed, brow furrowed in concentration. Then she rocked back on her heels and opened her eyes. She gave Joanna a silent nod. Joanna woke the rabbit again and nodded back.

Macaria killed the rabbit and Joanna brought it back half a dozen more times before Macaria's shoulders rounded forward in defeat. She shook her head as tears gathered in her eyes.

"I can't do this," Macaria groaned.

"Well, if you're going to be this weak-willed about it I may as well teach you how to take your own life now." Macaria pursed her lips. "If you cannot hold yourself together through one lesson, I can't imagine you'll be able to manage the rest of your training."

Macaria's head reared back and her mouth flew open in shock. She closed her jaw with an audible click.

"Maybe if you would actually tell me what to look for and teach me something," Macaria hissed, her eyes flashing. "We could stop torturing this animal and have dinner."

"Every death witch feels her power differently, Macaria," Joanna said in a firm, even voice. "Telling you what I feel would provide you no guidance, and might, in fact, hinder you from ever gaining control of your gift. But that still doesn't change the fact that you seem unwilling to try, to work. I wonder how your poor mother put up with your laziness all these years?" Joanna mused as she tilted her head to the side and regarded her student with a fierce eye.

"Leave my mother out of this," Macaria growled. "Wake the rabbit."

Without a word, Joanna resurrected the rabbit under Macaria's furious glare. Macaria reached out and touched the rabbit. This time, instead of wilting into death immediately the rabbit kicked and squealed for almost a minute before it died under her hand. Macaria's fury quickly shifted to horrified fear.

"What did I do wrong?" she cried.

"You didn't do anything wrong," Joanna said. "You finally seem to be developing something. Do you remember anything about what it felt like inside of you while the rabbit died?"

Macaria's eyes took on a faraway stare as she looked deep into herself and her memory. She shook her head and nodded to Joanna. "Wake the rabbit again, please."

This time when Joanna woke the rabbit it did not struggle or try to run away. It simply lay in Joanna's arms, trembling but still breathing.

Macaria reached out and laid her hand on the rabbit. Still, it breathed. She stroked her hand down its side. Still, it breathed. She scratched the creature behind its ears. Still, it breathed.

"Very good, Macaria," Joanna murmured. "You caught on much faster than many other students. Do you think you can remember what it felt like and use that to control yourself?"

Macaria nodded, her eyes wide.

"Good," Joanna said with a nod. "Now, kill this poor creature on purpose so we can have dinner. I'm positively starved."

After student and teacher finished preparing and eating dinner, they huddled close to the fire each wrapped in her own travel cloak and thoughts. Joanna seemed to be content with the silence and watched the flames of their small cook fire as if it told her stories. Macaria kept stealing furtive glances at her teacher.

"I am your teacher and I am supposed to answer your questions," Joanna said after some time. "So please ask them instead of acting like a skittish cat. I cannot teach you if I don't know where your knowledge is lacking."

Macaria snorted. "I think my knowledge is lacking in all things death witch-related."

Joanna gave her a sideways look with one side of her mouth quirked up. "I would not argue with you on that point."

"You could at least pretend I'm not an idiot for a minute or two," Macaria huffed, drawing her knees up to her chest.

"I never said you were stupid, child," Joanna said as she fed another small stick into the fire. "Merely unversed in the ways of the power you suddenly possess."

"It doesn't sound so bad when you put it that way," Macaria said as her shoulders loosened.

The quiet stretched on between them for a few more minutes.

"You never asked me your question," Joanna broke the silence.

"Only because I can't decide which one to ask first," Macaria said. "Mama prepared me to become one of the more common types of witches, but she never mentioned death witches. I know nothing."

Joanna nodded. "Thankfully, I don't have to undo a lot of false notions."

"That is one way of thinking of it." Macaria let out a bitter laugh and stroked her fingers over her hair. She stared into the fire with a furrowed brow and continued to fiddle with her braid.

Joanna regarded her student with a smile verging on fond. "You want to know if you can live a relatively normal life after you learn to bring your power under control. You wonder if you will be able to take a lover or a husband. You wonder if you will be able to have children."

Macaria's head jerked up. "How did you know?"

Joanna threw her head back and let loose a full-throated laugh that danced off through the trees into the dark beyond the firelight.

"Because I had exactly the same questions when I first came into my power," Joanna said as her eyes twinkled.

"Well?" Macaria asked, leaning forward eagerly.

"You will be able to take a lover or husband as you wish, assuming you can find one who will not fear who you are," Joanna began. "However, if he is skilled enough in the bedroom arts to sufficiently distract you, you may have to restart his heart when you lose your concentration."

Macaria flushed crimson as an expression of combined shock and awe crept over her face.

"Has that ever happened to you?" she whispered.

Joanna would not look directly at Macaria, but she smiled tenderly as she looked off in the dark of the forest.

"There are some things that are private, child, but you could say that Jakob was not unfamiliar with his heart being started and stopped."

Macaria covered her mouth as her eyes widened.

"Now, just remember that I am in full control of my power before you share that tidbit with anyone." Joanna tried to give Macaria a severe glare, but then she dissolved into a fit of giggles. Macaria soon found herself giggling in return. She noticed that when her teacher laughed she looked much younger.

Once the laughter subsided, Macaria asked, "What about children?"

Joanna sighed. "That is a thornier issue. Death witches have had children and most of the time everything turns out fine. The death touch doesn't seem to run in family lines. But sometimes..." Joanna paused and took a deep breath. "The mad witch who raised the long-dead was the daughter of a death witch." Joanna sighed. "The Council... discourages us from having children. We are not forbidden, but it is a dangerous thing."

Macaria nodded. "I know herbs to close the womb, both temporarily and permanently. My mother taught me that."

"Yes, we death witches make a point of being familiar with those ourselves."

They both watched the fire again in a more comfortable peace. Macaria broke the silence next.

"What will my final test be?" Macaria asked, still staring into the fire. "Mama told me all about the final tests that ended her apprenticeship, but I hardly think you'll be sending me on a three-day herb hunt with only a knife and my wits."

Joanna paused before she answered Macaria. "Once I am satisfied that you can control your death touch and that you can perform all the rites, rituals, and spells that go with our duties, you will kill me."

"What?" Macaria tore her eyes away from the fire.

"You will kill me, and then bring me back to life," Joanna continued. "Then your training will be complete, and you will take your oath as a death witch beholden only to the Polish Council of Witches."

"What if I can't bring you back?" Macaria asked in a stunned voice.

"Then the other death witches will hunt you down and bring you to heel," Joanna said. "Whether they feel they can keep you on a leash determines if you get to live." She lifted her head and fixed Macaria with a hard stare. "If you cannot bring me back at your final test, I suggest that you do not run. You should attempt to find another death witch as quickly as possible. She may be able to fix your error. Perhaps if she likes you, she'll help you cover it up. Then you can pass your final test on the second try and take your oath, and none but your mentor and your savior will be the wiser."

Macaria sat in stunned silence for several long minutes after Joanna turned back to the fire.

"What if I pass but then I don't want to swear fealty to the Council?" Macaria whispered.

"Then the Council I have already sworn fealty to will instruct me to kill you. They will consider you far too dangerous to wander about without being properly bound." Joanna's voice was soft. "Please don't make me do it. That is a death that has no grace or beauty."

Macaria nodded. "I promise."

Chapter Five

Joanna and Macaria arrived in Warsaw just after noon as the sun began its slow descent to the horizon. Joanna navigated the bustling streets with ease, Macaria trotting along in her wake with considerably less grace.

"How much longer?" Macaria whined. "My feet are so sore."

"Our Chapter House is just on the other side of the city," Joanna sighed. "We'll be there soon. And stop whining, not all of our Sisters are as patient as I am. You must mind your manners more." Under her breath Joanna murmured to herself. "Your mother did you no favors by being so indulgent."

Macaria paused and frowned. "If our Chapter House is on the other side, wouldn't it be faster to go through the city center?" She threw her hands up in the air. "We're walking miles extra going roundabout through the outskirts."

Joanna halted and whirled around. "I'm beginning to lose patience with you," she snapped. "Don't exaggerate. It's not miles extra." Joanna resettled her pack and set off again. Macaria rushed to keep up with her.

"Do you have any idea how crowded the city center is?" Joanna asked as Macaria drew even with her.

Macaria looked around at the scattered people they wove through. "This is the most people I've ever seen in one place. It can't be much more than this. There aren't enough people!"

"Hah!" Joanna barked. She stopped and caught Macaria's eyes. "The city center has three times or more people and it's nearly impossible to walk five feet without brushing up against someone. You have very good control for one so early in her training, but I can't trust you not to get distracted your first time in the city. I'd rather not spend half my first day back re-animating innocents and the other half explaining to the Council how I could let my apprentice accidentally kill half the city."

"Oh." Macaria's shoulders hunched in. "I'm sorry, I should have thought…"

"Yes, you must think," Joanna snapped. "If you don't think things through people die."

Macaria bit her lip and cast her eyes down. "Yes, ma'am," she murmured.

Joanna tilted her head to the side, her shoulders relaxing. "You should actually be proud."

Macaria looked up with a silent question in her eyes.

"We bring in most apprentices in the dead of night taking the straightest line from the wild to the Chapter House," Joanna said with a twinkle in her eye. "We don't allow them around people for months." Joanna leaned forward and whispered in Macaria's ear. "I have a feeling you are going to make me proud. We've not seen your like in generations."

Macaria did not complain again the rest of the way.

The Chapter House of the Polish death witches was a neat two-story stone house, only a hundred years old, tucked in a quiet quarter of Warsaw on a little-used side street. Joanna's step quickened as she turned the final corner. A single caw echoed down the street and a crow ghosted down on silent feathers, alighting on Joanna's shoulder.

"Yes, I'm home, Cień," she chuckled. "I'm sorry it took me so long." She bounded up the two steps to the front door, spots of color high on her cheeks.

"When do I get a crow of my own?" Macaria asked as Joanna fumbled in the bottom of her travel sack for the key.

"When one takes a liking to you." Joanna swung the door open and stepped over the threshold with a happy sigh. The house was quiet and dim. A cat lounging on the stairs leading up to the second floor interrupted its bath to chirp a greeting. Joanna shut the door behind Macaria but didn't divest herself of her traveling clothes. She headed deeper into the house.

"Does anyone else live here?" Macaria asked, trotting after Joanna. "Where are you going?"

"Every death witch in Poland maintains a room here," Joanna said over her shoulder. "But whether they are here or out on assignment is the question. I'll settle you into your room as soon as I've greeted someone."

Joanna stepped out of the back door of the house into a tiny fenced-in stable yard and headed straight for the small stable at the other end.

"Półmrok! Wiezór!" she called as she entered. Two coal-black horses stuck their heads over the stall doors and whinnied a greeting. Joanna dug in her travel sack and produced two apples. The horses' ears pricked forward and they eagerly shuffled their hooves in the hay.

Macaria put her hands on her hips. "We have horses? Why did we just spend two weeks walking through the forest when we could have ridden?"

"I have my reasons," Joanna murmured, leaning her forehead into Wiezór's.

"I'd like to hear them," Macaria grumped, crossing her arms across her chest.

Joanna's eyebrow quirked up as she flicked a glance at Macaria, but she answered. "Mostly, because of Cossacks. Horses would make us obvious and tempting targets. And it's easier to hide if you don't have to hide a large animal, too. The Partition has calmed things down somewhat, but it's not quite peaceful yet."

Oh, I..." Macaria dropped her arms.

"I'm not done yet," Joanna said crisply. "Półmrok and Wiezór also draw the hearse when a rich lord pays us to perform funerary rites. They do make quite the striking pair, don't they?" She stretched her arms out to rub both horses under the chin. "They need to be available at a moment's notice. Many of the folk who need us cannot afford to pay for our services, but the aristocracy can. They keep us fed so we can serve all of Poland. And when I received word that you existed, I was already traveling on foot on assignment." Joanna fixed Macaria with a gimlet stare. "Good enough?"

Macaria blushed and cast her eyes down. "Good enough."

"Welcome home, Koniec Lewandowski." A sandy-haired young man of perhaps fourteen emerged from the tack room that faced the stalls. "Koniec Mazur is in residence, but she is out with my mother getting the ingredients for dinner."

"So formal, Mitchell." Joanna chuckled as she scratched behind Wiezór's ears.

The young man shrugged and leaned against the tack room doorframe with a smile. "You usually want pomp and formality when there are new ears about." He nodded toward Macaria.

"Mitchell, meet my new apprentice, Macaria. Macaria, meet Mitchell, he is our stable hand and groundskeeper. His mother, Anna, is the Chapter House housekeeper." Joanna waved her hand vaguely in their direction as she turned her attention to Półmrok. "Go on and get to know each other."

Mitchell tipped an imaginary hat to Macaria and bowed. "Good afternoon, Mistress Macaria. I am Mitchell, of no family other than my mother. We were taken in by the generous witches of this house when I was but a bastard babe, and they've kindly allowed me to stay since I made myself useful."

Joanna guffawed. "You make it sound like a business transaction! You left out the part where we're lucky to have your mother because of how well she cares for us, and how every death witch in Poland loves you and considers her nephew."

Macaria bobbed a curtsey. "Macaria Niemiera, new apprentice."

"So, who did you kill?" Mitchell's eyes glittered and a little smirk turned up the corners of his lips.

"Don't be rude!" Joanna scolded, finally turning away from the horses. "She's not even been here an hour. She certainly hasn't learned the dark humor of the house yet."

A voice called out a greeting from across the stable yard. Joanna turned briskly and headed for the house.

"Ah, good," she said, motioning for Macaria to follow. "They're home. Time for you to meet another Sister and get settled in."

Macaria turned to follow Joanna but paused in the stable door.

"It was a cat," she said. "And I actually liked her."

"Oh." Mitchell blushed and shoved his hands in his pockets. "I'm sorry."

Macaria scurried after Joanna.

Joanna led Macaria into the kitchen and stillroom that spanned the back of the house. Two pleasantly plump women of indeterminate middle age unpacked baskets onto the long table that dominated the kitchen end of the room.

"Estera! Anna! I'm home!" Joanna caroled as she finally began to divest herself of her scarf, gloves, and travel cloak.

"Don't just leave your things everywhere. I don't want to have to go hunting when I do the wash," said the one with a twinkle in her eye.

"Darling! Good to see you. How did your assignment go?" said the other.

"I gave Jakub peace," Joanna said. "The rest of the story needs some wine and tears."

"Agata?" Estera asked.

"Part of it," whispered Joanna.

"I'm so sorry, dear," Estera murmured. "I know he was special to you." Silence took over the room.

"So, this is the new one?" Estera cleared her throat and pointed with her chin at Macaria as she sorted potatoes. "Where did you pick her up?"

"Out in the woods, small town," Joanna said. "Daughter of a hedgewitch." Joanna set her travel sack on the table and hunted through it. "Aha, here it is!" She pulled out a book and handed it to Anna. "I ran into a tinker on the road and he had the poetry book you've been looking for."

"How lovely! Thank you." Anna immediately flipped the book open and started scanning the pages.

Joanna chuckled. "Will dinner be late tonight? Sometimes I think we made a mistake teaching you how to read," she teased.

"Oh no," Anna said, not lifting her eyes from the pages. "I'd planned stew and some nice, crusty bread. I can do that while I read."

Estera put her hands on her hips as she approached Macaria, appraising her.

"I hope I can assume your mother taught you something about herb craft even if you weren't ready for spellwork?" she asked.

"Yes, ma'am." Macaria nodded. "Mama always assumed I would take her place, so she taught me everything."

Estera snorted. "I hardly think she taught you everything. She's only a hedgewitch after all."

Macaria opened her mouth to protest, but Estera held up a hand to forestall her.

"There's nothing wrong with hedgewitches and I'm sure your mother is a very talented one," Estera said. "There are just many things a hedgewitch doesn't need to know, so she can't have taught you everything."

Joanna's eyes sparkled. "You'll learn, Macaria. Estera can be just a bit pedantic."

"I don't see what's wrong with expecting people to be exact with their language," Estera pouted. "If you use the wrong word in a spell you can kill someone. It's best to stay in the habit of using just the right word." She nodded emphatically.

"Mama did say that the right words were important." Macaria gave Estera a small smile.

"See, the child understands!" Estera threw her hands into the air and stuck her tongue out at Joanna. She turned back to

Macaria. "I'm just pleased we are not starting with a blank slate, dear. It's good that you already have some knowledge. Welcome home."

Joanna laughed and picked up her bag. "I'll show Macaria her room so she can settle in before dinner."

Bare feet sounded on the stone floor leading to the kitchen, and a young woman paused in the doorway with both hands on the frame. Her loose dark hair floated like a cloud around her head. Her eyes were wide and wary. She scanned the room, sniffing the air. Her eyes settled on Macaria and she scampered over to her.

The strange girl circled Macaria three times, sniffing all the while. Her intense eyes roved all over her, as if trying to learn every curve of her body, every wrinkle of her clothes. She was so close that Macaria could feel the heat coming off of her body, but the girl never touched her. The girl stopped facing Macaria, her eyes boring into her. Their noses nearly touched.

"Tick tock. Mind the clock." The girl tilted her head to the side expectantly.

Macaria took a step back. "I'm sorry, what?"

The girl said again, "Tick tock. Mind the clock." She bounced on her toes and clutched her hands in front of her.

Macaria looked to Joanna. "Am I supposed to know what this means?"

Estera took the girl by the shoulders and pulled her a few steps back from Macaria. The girl looked at Estera and strained against her hands, shaking her head. "Tick tock? Mind the clock?"

"Not now, dear," Estera soothed and rubbed her shoulders.

"This is Lena," Joanna said to Macaria. "She is Zofia's daughter. She is… different."

Macaria crossed her arms over her chest and took another step back. "I can see that. Is her difference dangerous?"

"She has the mildest death touch we've ever seen," Joanna said. "She usually just puts people into a deep sleep. Once she put a man into a coma. We think she might have some touch of prophecy. When she was a small girl she woke screaming in the night the same prophecy the Cagliostro witches reported, something about a seventh daughter of a seventh daughter..."

"Tick tock, mind the clock! Tick tock, mind the clock!" Lena shouted, quivering in Estera's grip.

Joanna sighed. "Even without her foreknowledge of the Cagliostro Prophecy some of the things she says are unusual enough to seem like prophecy."

Lena yanked herself from Estera's grip and leapt at Macaria. She made as if to grab Macaria's shoulders, but stopped just short.

"Ticktockmindtheclock. Ticktockmindtheclock," she hissed. Her eyes searched Macaria's face, pleading for something, but Macaria didn't know what.

Macaria shook her head. "I'm sorry, I don't know what you want."

Lena burst into tears and sat down on the floor hard. She sobbed into her hands. "Tick tock. Mind the clock. Tick tock. Mind the clock."

Macaria gasped and reached forward, but then jerked her hands back. Estera crouched down next to Lena, rubbing her back and murmuring into her ear.

"I'm so sorry. I'm sorry." Macaria turned to Joanna, words tumbling out of her mouth. "What did I do? I didn't mean to upset her. I just don't know what she's talking about!"

Joanna held up her hand to stop Macaria's babbling. "We often don't know what Lena means when she speaks. You did nothing wrong." She frowned and rubbed her chin. "But let's try to remember her words. They might be important. I haven't seen her this upset since the Cagliostro Prophecy."

Estera helped Lena stand and led her, sobbing and hiccupping, from the room. The three women looked from one to another in silence. No one seemed sure of what to say for several long moments.

"I put fresh linens on her bed," Anna finally said with a shrug.

"You are a treasure, Anna," Joanna called over her shoulder as she led Macaria out of the kitchen and back to the front hall of the house. She hung her travel cloak on a peg and gestured for Macaria to do the same.

She pointed to the closed doors on either side of the hall. "That is the room the twins share; they are the oldest in the house and they are visiting family right now. And that is the room Olena and Parisa share, they are the next oldest. They aren't blood sisters, but they might as well be they are so close. They began training the same day decades ago and they've been inseparable ever since. They're on assignment helping some Ukrainian witches. We might wind up dragged into that."

"Dragged into what?" Macaria asked as they mounted the stairs.

"There have been signs that there might be an undiscovered death witch gone rogue." Joanna clucked her tongue and shook her head. "If that really is the case, we may all have to pull together to bring her to heel."

Joanna gestured down the hall of the second floor. "Everyone else has a room here; they aren't very big. My door is the second on the left if you need to come find me." She turned to climb a narrower set of stairs to the garret.

Typical of all garrets, the room was cramped and dim. Macaria and Joanna had to walk bent over except at the very center of the room. In one corner was a bed with the promised fresh linens, a bedside table with a small oil lamp and vase with sprigs of lavender, and an old, dark wood wardrobe. The other end of the room held a similar set of furniture, disused and covered with old sheets.

"All apprentices share the garret," Joanna said. "There are no others at this time, so while the room might not be the best, at least you don't have to share. When I was training there were four other girls in here."

Macaria surveyed the room. "How did you all fit?"

Joanna shrugged. "We were on top of each other all the time. It was a good thing we found each other agreeable company. Then Maaike left us, and after her Waiola..."

"Left you?"

Joanna straightened her shoulders. "I've told you before, not everyone who starts training finishes. Some are not suited for the life of a death witch." She smiled gently at Macaria. "I'll leave you some time to get settled."

After Joanna left, Macaria sat down on the bed and wondered if she would be one of the unsuitable girls or if she would eventually move downstairs.

Spring rain fell in a gentle patter against the windows as Joanna, Macaria, and Estera worked at a stone counter in the stillroom, sorting herbs and poultices.

Macaria sniffed a bundle of lavender. "This one isn't any good for healing anymore, but it still smells nice. Do you think Anna would want it to put with the stored linens?"

Estera let out a happy sigh.

"That's a lovely idea, Macaria," Joanna said. "We shouldn't waste anything even if it's not good for its original purpose."

"Have I mentioned yet how delightful it is that we don't have to teach you every little thing?" Estera grinned over bundles of sage.

"Only about three times," Macaria laughed. She was amazed by how comfortable she felt in the Chapter House of the death witches already.

"Speaking of training," Macaria said. "When do I begin?"

"You've already begun, Macaria. We did quite a bit on the road already," Joanna said.

"Well, yes, I know. But I thought we would begin a more intense regimen as soon as we got here." Macaria sniffed another bundle of lavender and nodded. She tucked it back into the drawer for medicinal lavender. "Isn't it critical to ensure I get my power under control as quickly as possible?"

Estera deliberately pushed her shoulder into Macaria's. Macaria jumped and pulled away with a gasp.

"If I hadn't been a death witch, you would have killed me with that bump," Estera said. "I could feel your gift, but mine was strong enough to counter it."

"One of the hardest tricks to master is constant control of your death touch," Joanna said. "Your control must be second nature, without thought. You mustn't be a danger to others even as you do the most innocuous task, like sorting herbs."

Macaria's eyes widened with understanding. "You've been training me this whole time."

"Indeed," Joanna said. "I am your mentor of record, however both Estera and I will be working with you, especially in the early stages. If there is an accident one of us will be close enough to correct it before there is any serious damage."

"It really is the most irritating part of training," Estera sighed. "Dying and waking, dying and waking… It upsets all of your rhythms and makes it hard to get a good night's sleep." She smiled at Macaria. "But you haven't killed me yet! It's very impressive for your first day in the house."

Macaria blinked and swallowed hard. "This will take some getting used to."

"The casual way we talk about death?" Joanna quirked up and eyebrow.

Macaria frowned. "Mama was more comfortable with death than any of the villagers, but even she didn't laugh about it or speak of it like going out to fetch eggs from the chicken coop."

Estera and Joanna looked at each other and laughed.

"It will come to you in time," Joanna said. "When death is such a constant part of all your days, it's hard not to make him your dear friend."

Macaria nodded. "What comes next? After I get myself under control?"

"We'll be training you the whole time, until your control comes," Joanna said. "You'll learn more about herbcraft and midwifery…"

"Midwifery?" Macaria interrupted. "What would a death witch do in a birthing room?"

"More than you would imagine…" Estera hung a fresh bundle of valerian to dry.

"We belong wherever the threshold between life and death is, Macaria. The birthing chamber is one of the most dangerous rooms a woman ever faces in her life," Joanna said. "So, we learn how to help healthy mothers have healthy babes, and we are there to help those who need us."

"Who needs us?"

"Some babies need a reminder to breathe or beat its wee heart," Estera said. "It's the duty that I love most. We deal with so much death and sickness, to hand a healthy babe to a mother when she would have otherwise buried…" Estera paused. "Well, that is a real joy."

Macaria straightened her shoulders. "Is that everything I need to learn about midwifery, or is there more?"

"We also help the mother," Estera said. "As Joanna said, giving birth is a dangerous exercise. There are a great many things that can go wrong. Sometimes we may need to restart the mother's heart, and sometimes we let her soul slip out so we have a few minutes to work on her body without having to worry about the reflexive pain responses. Then we can draw her soul back in and the child doesn't have to grow up motherless."

"There are some rewards for all the difficulties," Joanna said with a gentle smile.

"What else?" Macaria looked from Joanna to Estera. "What else do I have to learn?"

Joanna turned back to the herbs on the stone table, a small smile on her lips. "You will also learn the deeper herbcraft. We only deal the death touch when we must. Some who request our talents can be cured of what ails them and live instead of dying."

Macaria nodded. "I'm still not certain I am suited to this life, but I will keep learning until I am certain of my path."

"That is all we can ask of you," Joanna said laying her hand over Macaria's. She drew it back with a sharp intake of breath. "Perhaps you should take a few moments to calm yourself. If I hadn't been prepared you would have killed me just now, even though I am a death witch."

"Come, sit over here." Estera gestured to a stool in the corner of the room. "I have some breathing exercises I can teach you. I had a harder time learning control than Joanna did. I had to learn a few more calming tricks."

The rain continued for several days and Półmrok developed a cough. On the third afternoon, Macaria wrapped her travel cloak around herself to make the dash across the small stableyard and deliver a crock of warm stew to Mitchell from his mother. She found Mitchell in Półmrok's stall scratching him behind the ears. Wiezór stretched his head over his stall door snuffling his concern for his stablemate.

"I have something for you to eat," Macaria said as she held up the crock.

"Thank you," Mitchell said. "You can set it on that hay bale."

Macaria backed away a few steps after she set the stew down. "How is he doing?"

"He's over the worst of it." Mitchell shut the stall door behind him. "He'll be fine in another day or two. I'm surprised Joanna isn't out here checking in on him herself."

"She's been called to consult on the birthing of some lordling's mistress, who knows how long she'll be. Babies have their own time." Macaria frowned. "She has been a little on edge the last few days."

Mitchell nodded as he dug into the stew. "I'm not surprised. She's been out here as much as she could, but with your training she can't be here as much as she would like."

"Why are these horses so important to her?" Macaria asked.

"They're all she has left of her blood family," Mitchell said softly.

"What do you mean?"

"When Joanna's power manifested she accidentally killed her mother as they were washing dishes," Mitchell said. "Then, when she tried to tell her father in her panic, she killed him too. They weren't a witch family, so they had no idea what was going on. By the time Parisa got the call and came to get her, Joanna's parents were too far gone to be brought back."

"That's awful! She didn't have any brothers or sisters?"

"She has three brothers and five sisters. Her eldest brother took over the farm. Joanna was the oldest daughter, so the second oldest girl took over raising the younger children." Mitchell took a bite of stew his eyes focused on some middle distance.

"And they just cast her out? But she had no control over getting her power."

"No, they welcomed her back to the farm after she was done her training. She went home for a visit after one of her assignments a few years ago. She's quite fond of her nieces. While she was there, one of their carting mares foaled these two." Mitchell waved his spoon at Półmrok and Wiezór. "But twins are hard on horses. The mare died and her foals were still. Joanna brought all three of them back. Her brother couldn't understand how she would "waste" her ability to resurrect a living being on horses when she wouldn't use it on her parents."

Macaria brought her hands to her mouth and whispered, "Oh, no."

"He was going to kill all three of them because he said it was unnatural they were alive," Mitchell continued. "Joanna begged for their lives. He said she could have them as long as she never returned to the farm again." He set his empty crock aside with a sigh. "There wasn't enough room here for all three of them after Półmrok and Wiezór weaned. So, their mother is a delivery horse for a dairy farm to the east of town. We see her sometimes."

"Poor Joanna," Macaria murmured.

"Most of the witches in this house have a sad story like that. Many people find death witches hard to accept." Mitchell barked a short laugh. "Even my mother and I have a sad story like that."

Macaria tilted her head to the side. "What is your sad story?"

"My mother was a chambermaid for a lord living in Krakow. He was hosting foreign lords for trade discussions. One particular lord took an interest in my mother and convinced her that he truly loved her. He promised that he'd marry her and take her home with him to England as soon as the negotiations were over." Mitchell's face hardened. "When he sailed back across the Channel he abandoned my mother with me already growing in her belly. She hid her pregnancy as long as she could, but eventually her employer found out and tossed my mother onto the street."

"Oh, Anna…" Macaria glanced back toward the house.

Mitchell drew himself up and smiled. "But my mother is a strong woman. She found a way to survive. I was only three when she secured employment here at the Chapter House; I don't really remember anything about life on the streets."

"What about your father?" Macaria asked.

"What about him?" Mitchell shrugged. "He probably doesn't know I exist, and he probably doesn't care either. All I have of my father is my name and my hair." Mitchell ran his hand through his sandy hair. "Everything else is from my mother."

"How did he give you a name if he doesn't know you exist?"

"Mama named me after him," Mitchell explained. "He was Lord James Mitchell, from somewhere in England. Mama told me where when I was younger, but after a while we both just tried to forget. There wasn't any reason to remember."

Chapter Six

The smell of smoke and frightened whinnies of the horses woke Macaria in the wee hours of the morning. Lena stood at the foot of her bed, wringing her hands.

"Tick tock. Mind the clock. Tick tock. Mind the clock," she muttered.

Macaria grabbed her shawl and stumbled down the garret stairs calling for Joanna and Estera, Lena on her heels. The older witches were both already in the hall, tugging their shawls tightly over their nightdresses and running for the stairs.

Anna stood in the back door with her hands over her mouth, the light of flickering flames dancing over her face. Estera pulled her out of the doorway by the shoulders, then Joanna and Macaria could see the full extent of the calamity.

The thatched roof of the stable was completely engulfed in flame. They could hear the horses screaming in terror. Two shadowy male figures brawled in the stable yard limned in firelight. As they twisted and grappled with each other, Macaria caught shadowy glimpses of their faces. One was Mitchell, and the other was a young man who looked familiar but that Macaria couldn't quite place.

"We have to get the horses out!" Joanna shouted as she leaped into the yard.

Estera grabbed Anna and pulled her into the yard after her. "Get the gate open," she instructed. "And rouse the neighbors. If we don't get the fire out half the city could burn!"

Estera's words seemed to stir Anna from her frozen horror. She scurried for the gate in the stable yard wall.

Estera grabbed Macaria's hand and pulled her toward the stable. "Let's help Joanna with the horses." She glanced over her shoulder at Lena, still standing in the kitchen doorway. "Lena, stay there!"

Lena sat down on the threshold, wrapping her arms around herself and muttering. She fixed her eyes on the fire.

Macaria, Joanna, and Estera started to dash across the yard to the stable. They were halfway there when the strange man roared and threw Mitchell down to the ground. Mitchell's head bounced on the stone. He lay there, groaning and shaking his head, trying to lever himself up.

"Foul witch!" The stranger threw himself in front of the women. He drew an axe from his belt and pointed it at Joanna. "You must pay for what you took from me!"

The fire flared up and Macaria saw his face more clearly. A memory slid into place. This was the young man who had consoled Agata when Joanna gave Jakub the final comfort.

Joanna drew herself up and lifted her chin. "Your father gave his word that the Polish Witches Council and I would be held blameless, Stefan. Please step aside."

"Don't you dare use my name, witch! You have no power over me!" Stefan roared. He swung his axe clumsily, the wide arc not even coming close to Joanna. "You bewitched my father, but you will not bewitch me."

"I held no sway over your father." Joanna kept her voice calm and low. "He was in his right mind when he asked for peace."

"Lies!" Stefan shrieked. "I will kill you and everything you love. This whole foul house will burn before you taste the flames of hell!"

Mitchell finally stumbled to his feet and tottered to Joanna's side. "You'll have to kill me before you lay a hand on her."

"That can be arranged," Stefan snarled. He swung his axe again. Mitchell stepped out of the way easily.

"You need to work on your aim," Mitchell taunted. "We move a bit more than trees, bumpkin."

"We'll keep him occupied," Joanna hissed. "Get the horses out." She pushed Estera and Macaria toward the stable. Grabbing Macaria's hand, Estera ran. Macaria stumbled behind her.

"But shouldn't we help…" Macaria began.

Estera cut her off. "Joanna and Mitchell can take care of themselves. We get the horses out, then we help."

Estera and Macaria crouched low, trying to stay under the smoke. It was impossible. The ceiling of the stable was nothing but a sheet of rippling flame. Macaria coughed and choked. Her lungs ached. In their stalls, the horses screamed, battering the walls and doors with frantic hooves. Estera gestured for Macaria to go right while she took the stall on the left.

She leaned in a wheezed in Macaria's ear, "Use your shawl to cover his eyes."

"Why don't we just open the doors?" Macaria gasped back. "Won't they just run into the yard? Anna's at the gate and can keep them from running into the street."

Estera shook her head. "Sometimes we need young minds to see the simpler way." She cackled. "Let's do it together."

They undid the latches at the same time, hiding behind the doors to protect themselves from the terrified horses' hooves. Półmrok and Wieżór galloped into the stable yard, screaming all the way. Macaria and Estera snatched halters and leads off the hooks and raced after them.

Macaria gasped and drew in a great lungful of air as she emerged from the stable. Even though it was still hot and full of ash, it felt positively clean and cool compared to the air inside. The horses danced in the stable yard, trying to stay away from Stefan and Joanna. Macaria wondered where Mitchell was, seeing only the two figures in the firelight.

Macaria and Estera reached for Półmrok and Wiezór. The horses reared and whinnied. Anna scuttled over from the gate to help them soothe the horses. She sang a lullaby like she would for a fussy child. The horses stopped rearing and turned their ears to her. They still pranced and shifted, but they allowed Estera and Macaria to put their halters on.

Macaria handed Półmrok's lead to Anna. "Get them somewhere safe. I'll go help Joanna." She disappeared into the thickening smoke before either could protest.

It didn't take long for Macaria to discover what happened to Mitchell. He lay on the stones of the stable yard clutching his belly. Blood and viscera seeped between his fingers. His face was pale and his breath came in short gasps. A small cloud of nyxies hovered over him. Joanna and Stefan circled each other, coughing from the smoke. Joanna danced back to avoid another swipe from Stefan's bloody axe.

Macaria knelt next to Mitchell. His skin was clammy. Turning his head slowly, he wheezed. "Help her," he choked out, his pupils wide.

"I'll kill you just like I killed your boy," Stefan panted. "And then I'll kill every other filthy witch in this house."

"Stefan, think!" Joanna coughed so hard she nearly doubled over. "Don't make me do something I'll regret."

"How can you regret anything when you have no soul?" Stefan growled. "You killed a man you claimed to love."

"I did love you father!" Joanna protested.

"Liar!" Stefan lunged again. Joanna barely avoided his axe this time.

Macaria set her jaw. "Sometimes a younger mind can see a simpler way." She launched herself at Stefan.

Macaria grabbed him from behind, wrapping her arms around his waist. She only made him stumble, but she wasn't trying to knock him from his feet. Not yet. Stefan grunted in surprise and tried to twist himself from Macaria's grasp. Macaria held fast. She closed her eyes and exhaled, letting her power flow with her breath. With her power came red-hot fury.

Stefan dropped like a stone.

Macaria yanked her arms out from under Stefan's dead weight. She scrambled back to Mitchell.

"It's alright," she huffed. "Joanna is safe. Stay with us." Macaria stroked his hair away from his sweaty forehead. She shooed fluttering nyxies from his face. Macaria looked back over her shoulder for Joanna. Joanna stood, frozen, her mouth open. "Get over here! We have to save him!" Macaria's voice cracked.

Joanna was at her side in a moment. She gently pulled Macaria's hands away from Mitchell, then settled his head in her lap. She stroked his forehead and cheeks, humming softly.

"Is this a new spell? What can I do?"

"There is nothing we can do." Joanna choked and tears began to slide down her cheeks.

"No. No, no." Macaria shook her head and reached for Mitchell's wounds. "There has to be something."

Joanna grabbed her by the wrists and wrenched her hands away. "There is nothing we can do." Her voice trembled. "Even our power has limits. He's lost too much blood."

"Can't we sew him up? Like we do for the women in childbirth? And then bring his soul back?" Macaria turned her desperate eyes to Joanna.

"No." Joanna's voice was so soft Macaria could barely hear her. "His body won't be able to make enough new blood in time. All we would do is prolong his pain."

"But can't we…"

"No." Joanna's voice was firm. "This is all we can do." She leaned forward and kissed him on the forehead. Mitchell was gone. Macaria tore her eyes away from the nyxies settling on his still form.

"We could have…" Macaria wailed.

"We could have what? Prolonged his pain? Turned him into the walking dead?" Joanna snapped. "Don't you think I wanted to save him?" Joanna bowed her head. Her tears fell on Mitchell's cooling cheeks. "We can't fix everything, Macaria. Sometimes the only thing we can do is let the Universe take its course." She looked up, her eyes red from smoke and tears. "This is the very hardest lesson you will have to learn."

The mid-morning breeze began to clear the pall of smoke hanging over the Chapter House and stable. The fire was out. Neighboring buildings only suffered a few minor burns and some scorching. The din of the neighborhood fighting the fire together made the hush settling over the streets now seem deeper.

Macaria, Joanna, Estera, and Lena sat on a bench against the house, ash smeared across their faces, hands, and bare feet. Soot stained their nightdresses and only Lena still had her shawl. Mitchell and Stefan lay in the cellar under the house, both already wrapped in their winding sheets. Anna slept in her bed with help from catnip tea and soft caresses from Lena.

The women on the bench all stared at the badly damaged stable across the yard. It would not be habitable for some time. Półmrok and Wiezór were stabled with an innkeeper two streets over. He was happy enough to care for the horses without payment, for now. His wife was pregnant, a surprise, and she was of an age that increased the danger of the birthing room. Their inn was moderately successful, but not so much to afford the attendance of a death witch at the birth. For them at least, the fire brought a blessing.

Joanna sighed and leaned her head back against the house, closing her eyes. Macaria leaned forward, resting her elbows on her knees and bowing her head.

"What are we going to tell the Council?" Macaria croaked, her voice harsh from the smoke.

Joanna didn't open her eyes or move. She said, "It was an accident. You've barely started your training. A man attacking us and setting our stable on fire would cause many a witch to forget her control."

"But I…" Macaria tried to interrupt but Joanna ignored her.

"You will appear before the Council and be appropriately contrite. You will be tearful and eager to make amends for your accident. You will tell them you were in fear for your life, that you were in fear that he would kill everyone in the house."

"But I did it on purpose!" Macaria cried. "I didn't lose control. I meant it. And I'm not sorry."

Joanna's eyes flew open. Her head snapped around to Macaria. "It. Was. An accident." She spat out the words.

"But…" Macaria protested.

"Macaria," Estera said in a flat voice. "Do you know what the Council would do to you if they found out you killed a man on purpose without proper forethought and sanction from the Council?"

"No." Macaria's cringed, her shoulders rounding in.

"To begin with, they will kill you." Estera was cold and matter of fact. "Then they will call your mother before a Tribunal. They will want to know how she raised a daughter who could kill so casually. If they are not satisfied with her answers, they will punish her."

Macaria's head snapped up and she gasped.

"Do you think Stefan would have hesitated to kill Joanna? To kill any of us who got in his was way?"

Macaria swallowed hard. "No."

"Then why throw your life away? You did the right thing to protect us. And now we are protecting you." Estera fixed Macaria with gimlet eyes. "It was an accident." She settled back against the wall.

Joanna closed her eyes and leaned back against the house again. "It was an accident."

"It was an accident," Macaria echoed. She imitated her mentor's posture. "And I'm sorry."

Lena looked down the line of women and nodded emphatically. She settled her back against the wall with a sigh and murmured, "Tick tock. Mind the clock."

Epilogue

It was spring again and Macaria was eighteen the next time she saw her mother. Elzbieta still lived in the same neat little cottage at the edge of the village, still served the same families. As Macaria walked up to the cottage, travel pack over one shoulder and a crow of her own on the other, she noted that there were more medicinal herbs in the front flower boxes than there used to be. She frowned. Were the people sicker, or was her mother finally starting to show her age and cutting back on trips into the forest to gather the herbs wild?

Macaria paused before the front door. The last time she'd been here she wouldn't have had a second thought about walking right in. But it had been so long since this had been her home and so much had changed. The crow on her shoulder cawed softly.

"I know she still loves me, Kumpel," she murmured. "But will she ever feel safe around me?"

The door flew open as she raised her fist to knock on her mother's door. Elzbieta stood on the threshold, smiling with tears streaming down her cheeks. She threw her arms open wide. Macaria stepped into that familiar embrace and laid her cheek on her mother's shoulder. She let out a sigh she felt like she'd been holding for years.

Elzbieta held her out and looked her daughter up and down. Her eyes stopped on the crow still perched firmly on Macaria's shoulder. "It is done? You are..."

"Yes, Mama," Macaria said. "My training is complete. I am a full-fledged Koniec, sworn to the service of the Polish Witches Council." She stepped forward and kissed her mother twice on her cheek, murmuring, "good-bye and hello." Elzbieta let out a little gasp and clutched her daughter tight again.

"Are you on your way to an assignment? Do you have time for tea?" Elzbieta asked when she let her go.

"Better than that," Macaria grinned. "Since I am only just done training and officially sworn, I get a month before they can send me on assignment. And I might be idle even longer than that if there are no assignments to give me."

"Well, then," her mother said as she threaded her arm through Macaria's. "We have time to catch up. We'll have tea and you can help me sort and store the herbs I've been drying."

"It's good to be home," Macaria said with a sigh.

"You know," Elzbieta said as they crossed the threshold arm in arm. "Your Aleksy still asks about you all the time. He has not married...."

"Mama," Macaria said in a shocked tone. "He was never my Aleksy."

Elzbieta *harrumph*ed as she put on the kettle. "Not to hear him tell it."

With a silent hand signal, Macaria directed her crow to fly out the open window over her mother's workbench and do as he wished. She placed her travel bag in the corner and hung her cloak on the peg by the door. She then settled herself at her mother's table, following her bustling with fond eyes.

"I will need to go herb hunting tomorrow," Elzbieta said over her shoulder. "Perhaps you could have Aleksy over for a visit."

"Mama!" Macaria blushed and ducked her head. "Aleksy... Aleksy should find himself a nice village girl and settle down. I don't want to get in the way of that."

"Just because you don't want him forever doesn't mean you shouldn't have some fun and maybe get yourself a daughter out of it." Elzbieta laid teacups and a small pot of honey on the table.

"A child..." Macaria said with a sigh. "A child would be inadvisable at this time."

Elzbieta raised an eyebrow. "So, I am never to have a grand-daughter to bounce on my knee?"

Macaria sighed again. "Mama, there are some things I'm not allowed to tell you about, well, what I do. And some of those things make children something the Council discourages." She looked up as her mother's frowning face, full of sadness and she hurried on. "It doesn't mean I'll never have children, just that I have to plan carefully. And the careful plan says that now is not the time."

It was Elzbieta's turn to sigh. "Alright, I trust you to make the right choice, sweetling."

"Thank you, Mama."

Elzbieta pulled the singing kettle off the hob. "Just know that if you do have a child, and her timing is less than convenient, I can always watch her here when you need to go off on assignment."

"Oh, Mama..."

She set down the kettle and took her daughter's face in her hands. She kissed her on both cheeks and murmured, "Welcome home, my child."

An excerpt from

THE CLOCKWORK WITCH

Chapter I

*In Which We Enter the Witching World
of London Society and Meet Arabella*

The half-drunk glass of lemonade in her hand grew warm as Arabella watched the other guests from a small alcove nearly completely shrouded by a voluminous potted palm. She was sure the decorator meant it to be used by discrete young couples, but Arabella found it just as useful to get away from the uncomfortable stares and whispers. She watched partygoers swirl and laugh across marble floors. Brass and crystal chandeliers cast butter-soft candlelight over the merriment while a string quartet played in the background. The tall arched windows all around the room appeared black as the interior light blinded everyone to the more gentle light of the moon and stars. Arabella sighed as she tugged the low neckline on her lavender satin evening gown. It didn't fit quite right and the color was just ever so slightly off, the wrong contrast with her dark brown hair and pale blue eyes, but it was a hand-me-down from her mother and tailoring could only do so much.

Arabella may have found the party more exciting, and not tortuous at all, if she had not thought of herself as barren, completely devoid of magic. If she could just perform a simple scrying spell, if she could send or receive a thought, she might not feel like an outcast. Her eyes drifted half shut as one of her fondest recurring fantasies flitted through her mind's eye. In it she stepped out from behind the potted palm and plucked a fan from a nearby lady's hand with her telekinesis. Her imaginary self fanned her warm cheeks with the gaily-colored feathers while she discussed the intricacies of levitation with the other young scions of the London Houses. But she could do none of these things. She felt surrounded by people who either pitied her or were disgusted by her. At least she imagined it so and suppressed a shudder. She was a daughter of Blackstone House, seventh daughter of Minerva Vivienne Sortilege, the Lady Blackstone herself and Grande Dame of the English Council of Witches. Her other six sisters were all accomplished witches in their own right. In fact, the Sortilege bloodline of Blackstone House had not produced a Cassus, a woman born into a witch family with no talent for magic, in over 300 years. That is until she, Arabella Helene Sortilege, the humiliation of the Sortilege line and Blackstone House itself, was born.

"Someone might mistake you for a jungle cat, peeking out from behind those fronds like that," came a voice from behind her.

Arabella jumped, but relaxed when she realized it was her elder sister Rowena, the fifth-born daughter and the only real friend she had in her constrained little world. Rowena's coloring—rich auburn hair and deep brown eyes—was a near perfect echo of their mother, right down to her creamy porcelain skin. The deep hunter green of her plush velvet gown suited her perfectly and set off her witches' robes with flair, but then Rowena could afford to buy her own gowns. She was already drawing her stipend as an active member of the Council.

"You shouldn't scare people like that, Ro," Arabella laughed as she sipped from her glass. "I don't think your healing spells are up to restarting my heart yet."

"How would you know, Ari? I've been studying hard." Rowena jostled her sister's shoulder with her own and began to scrutinize the crowd herself. "Anything interesting?"

Arabella shrugged. "Just the usual, as far as I can tell. You?"

Rowena scanned the assembly with eyes half shut and the tip of her tongue tracing her bottom lip. "All the witches are shielding," she sighed. "Except Lady Wentworth, but she's in her cups anyway, so just the usual."

"Picking up anything from her?" Arabella tried to sound casual.

Rowena blushed. "Nothing you want to hear."

"Very much just the usual." Arabella's mouth thinned out to a hard line.

"Ari, don't take it so hard. Lady Wentworth is a lush and a gossip. Her opinion isn't worth much of anything." Rowena stroked her sister's arm from shoulder to elbow.

"Her opinion might not be worth much, but she's thinking the same thing everyone else is thinking. 'Poor little brown bud, such a disgrace, a stunted vine spoiling an otherwise lovely garden,'" Arabella's voice mocked in a sing-song tone.

"Ari…"

"What about the ordinary people?" Arabella interrupted her. "Can you hear anything from them?"

Rowena looked over the crowd for a moment and then pointed out an older, heavy woman in more lace than anyone but a very young girl should wear. "She's practically shouting."

"What is she thinking?"

Rowena shrugged. "She's trying to figure out who she can get to marry her daughters, who snubbed her and who she should snub, what she should order up from her cook for breakfast. Do mundane women ever think of anything else?"

"What else can they think of, Ro? They're not supposed to have jobs and their husbands rule everything, even their children. What else do they have to think about but marriages and snubs and menus?

"They're almost as useless as I am," Arabella's voice was soft and nearly lost in the chatter of the party.

Rowena sighed as she crossed her arms over her stomach and held her elbows close. Both sisters looked out over the room in silence. The colors of the gay party whirled around them, but never touched them with their merriment. Every witch who was worth her broom was there, as well as most of the more important alchemists, Lords from Parliament, and their wives.

"I wonder if Father is here," Arabella broke the silence.

"Probably not," said Rowena. "You know he avoids any event that Mother even might attend."

"Yes, but this is so special," said Arabella.

Bartholomew Westerfeld had gathered them all together to preview what he claimed was a great wonder before he showed it at The Great Exhibition. No one knew precisely what he was going to show and the gossip was running rampant. Would it be something to calm the growing unrest overseas, especially in the Crimea? Or perhaps it would be something to finally lift the horrible famine that had gripped the Irish people for so long. Mr. Westerfeld would not drop the slightest hint, and seemed to revel in the attention as everyone continued to guess.

Rowena shrugged. "Father's given his regrets for more important events before. He might have sent Henry or John in his stead. It would be nice to see our brothers again." Rowena craned her neck to observe every corner of the room.

Arabella opened her mouth to say something, but snapped it shut again as she saw Jessamine and Josephine approaching.

"It's time," Jessamine began.

"Mother wants you to come now," Josephine finished for her.

The twins regarded Arabella and Rowena with the bright blue eyes they had inherited from their father, faces unreadable. The twins were always inscrutable. They were absolutely alike in all ways, from their curly brown locks to their unnerving silences, except for one thing. Jessamine showed an affinity for fire magic while Josephine had more talent for the water magic arts. Even the wisest of crones could not explain the differences in the girls' magic. Twins were rare enough, but when they came their magic was usually linked in some way, not diametrically opposite, as it was with Jessamine and Josephine, the third- and fourth-born daughters to the Lady Blackstone. Even their Aunts, the twins Leanore and Lorena just one generation prior, had shared magical proclivities. Both had been talented earth witches.

"Well, I suppose we shouldn't dally now that we've been summoned," Arabella sighed. "Let's go."

"It'll be fine, Ari." Rowena squeezed her hand. "In fact, it might even be fun."

Arabella raised an eyebrow. "I'd settle for not a disaster."

As the girls started to make their way across the room to where their mother held court, along with Arabella's eldest sisters, Vivienne, Amelia, and Elizabeth, Jessamine and Josephine clasped hands together and grinned at each other. "It's time!" they chimed together.

"You said that already," Rowena frowned. "We're going, we're going."

Jessamine and Josephine simply put their heads together and giggled, unseemly behavior at their age and in a public venue.

Rowena leaned in and whispered into Arabella's ear as they walked arm and arm, "I swear, sometimes I think they're just trying to make everyone cross out of sheer perversity."

Arabella had to stifle a giggle, biting her lower lip, as they arrived at where their mother was standing. All four girls sank into neatly executed curtseys and bowed their heads to their mother.

"Is there something humorous you'd like to share with the rest of us, Arabella?" Minerva Sortilege asked.

"No, ma'am," said Arabella, curtseying again. "It was just a stray thought, unsuitable for such company."

"I see," said her mother. "Perhaps you should work harder at focusing on more appropriate thoughts in public, give me *something* to be proud about."

Arabella bowed her head, trying to hide her flaming cheeks. "Yes, Mother," she murmured.

Her eldest sister, Vivienne, presumed heir to both Blackstone House and the position of the Grande Dame, echoed their mother's frown at Arabella. Amelia, the next eldest, glanced at Vivienne and schooled her features in a perfect imitation.

Elizabeth, the sixth-born sister, just one year older than Arabella, covered the lower half of her face with her fan and tittered, her eyes gleaming.

"That will be quite enough, Elizabeth." Minerva quieted her daughter with a single frosty glance. "Gather around, ladies, we will go in together."

Minerva Sortilege turned from her daughters to face the ballroom, sweeping her burgundy satin skirts about with the practiced twitch of one hand. Her black velvet robes, open at the front and gathered at the shoulders, as all witches' robes were, showed the cunning cut of her ball gown and shimmered in a graceful fall from her shoulders to the floor, ending in a small, tasteful train. The arcane and esoteric symbols of the proud vocation of witchery were stitched all over the fabric, glowing and glimmering in response to the power the Lady Blackstone held. She was the most powerful witch in all of England, quite possibly the world. All eyes turned to her; every witch in the room envied her power. Minerva Sortilege kept her face schooled in the pleasant neutrality that such social situations required, but those who knew her could see the tell-tale downward tug at the corners of her lips.

Vivienne aligned herself at her mother's right shoulder, one respectful step back. Her ball gown of cobalt blue complimented her robes of deep charcoal velvet, which were not as elaborate as her mother's, nor did they shimmer and glow as much, but her robes still outshone most of the witches in the room. She would not assume her mother's mantle simply because of preference or birth, Vivienne was powerful enough in her own right to earn it. In another move only noticed by the Sortilege women, Vivienne's hand fluttered for a moment over her stomach before she dropped it by her side. This would probably be the last social event she would attend before sequestering herself at the family home in Boscastle to await the birth of her first child. Her husband, Nathanial Moreland, was already there making sure that everything was ready for her return. At thirty-one, she would be considered old for a first child if she were an ordinary woman, but since witches lived longer than most, hers was a very appropriate age.

Amelia settled herself at her sister's shoulder, arranging her dove gray robes with a less graceful hand than her sister or her mother, but she still drew her shoulders up and lifted her chin with pride. Josephine and Jessamine arrayed themselves to their mother's left, still holding hands and watching Arabella with their unnerving stare. Josephine's red velvet robes gave off the banked heat of her not insignificant power in fire magic, while Jessamine's blue velvet gave off the soothing cool of water. Between them the air bent and warped, sending up fitful gouts of steam, but the twins appeared unconcerned even as the party guests closest to them took a step back. Minerva glanced at them and sighed, and Arabella noticed a slight furrow in her brow that she imagined was her mother sending her wayward daughters a shielded thought to tamp down their emotions and get a hold of themselves. The Sortilege name might allow them latitudes not granted to other witches, and much more freedom than the average woman, but scalding their host's guests would almost certainly require significant apologies. The twins broke off staring at Arabella, the heat and steam subsiding, and nodded to their mother, lips twitching around the words of the unspoken apology they thought to her.

Elizabeth, Rowena, and Arabella stood shoulder to shoulder in a line behind their older and more powerful sisters. Rowena's purple velvet robes announced that she was still undecided about where to focus her talents, much to her mother's consternation, while Elizabeth's very pale gray velvet showed a low level of magical power and control, at least compared to her mother and sisters. In most other witch families, she would have been considered average. If Arabella had not been standing there, in only a ball gown and no robes at all, Elizabeth would be viewed as the embarrassment of the Sortilege line. But given that Elizabeth was only eighteen, there was at least some hope that her powers might yet grow with practice and hard work. Arabella had no such hope. The most powerful witches manifested their power at a very early age, Vivienne was levitating her toys before she could walk, and even the most average of witches began to manifest her powers with the onset of puberty. At seventeen, Arabella was well past hope that she would suddenly bloom into the witch her mother always wanted her to be.

All eyes in the room focused on the most important witches in the land. Minerva looked back to ensure all of her daughters were in their proper places. She gave each of her eldest four a slight nod while her youngest three received a barely perceptible frown. The frown deepened when her eyes fell on Arabella, becoming noticeable to even those outside of the Sortilege women. From the corners of her eyes, Arabella could see fans lift in front of ladies' lips and she imagined she could feel their whispers crawl up and down her spine. Hidden in the folds of her robe, Rowena reached out and twined her fingers around Arabella's and squeezed.

Eyes front and shoulders back, Minerva began to stride across the ballroom to where Bartholomew Westerfeld stood in front of the locked door to another ballroom that held what he swore was a wonder for the ages. Her daughters followed behind in tight formation. As they passed, witches and alchemists alike bowed and curtseyed. Even members of Parliament inclined their heads in respect.

Halfway across the room, three witches stepped into the path of Lady Blackstone and her daughters. The room seemed to gasp with one voice. Their robes were clean, but worn thin and only shining dully. The lead witch wore the deep blue of strong water magic, while the two that flanked her wore paler grays for middling general magic. Their ball gowns were of a fashion that had come and passed at least ten years ago. Each one was slender to the point of being sickly, with bright red hair and freckles dusted across ivory skin—Irish witches, all.

Minerva raised an eyebrow and looked pointedly past them. The lead witch raised her chin and kept her fists balled by her side, standing her ground.

"Sister," sighed Minerva. "If you do not mind, I have an appointment to keep."

"Sister," said the lead witch. "I have come to ask your favor and I will not move until I hear your answer."

Minerva's jaw tightened. "This is not the place to discuss such matters. There will be a session of the Council next month and you can address any concerns to me then."

"Grande Dame," the witch's voice cracked. "I have been trying to be heard at the Council for over a year now. I have been given no choice but to seek you here."

Minerva frowned and her eyebrows pinched together. "Remind me to speak to the Secretary about hearing petitions in a timely manner," she murmured to Vivienne, who nodded.

"Well, Sister," Minerva said. "Tell me who you are and what you are about so we can get on with the festivities of the evening."

The water witch took a deep breath and shut her eyes for a moment. Behind her, the other two clasped hands and bit their lips, exchanging glances.

"I am Shannon O'Reilley and I have come to speak for all the Irish witches, well, for all of Ireland, really. We're starving, Sister. Even though our fields grow, our children die from hunger. The English landlords require all but our potatoes, and those crops are failing from blight. Every earth witch we have has failed to cure the blight, and died in the trying. We have no one with earth powers left. Please, aid us so we can feed our families again. Or use your influence to convince the landlords to let us keep enough of what we grow for them to feed our children and old people." All three witches had tears in their eyes.

"Perhaps you are overstating the problem. I have heard recent reports of the blight easing," said Minerva with a frown. "However it stands, there are no earth witches to spare. I am sorry, but you will have to find some other way to deal with the blight."

"Please, Grande Dame," Shannon pleaded. "We've tried everything, we need your help. We have managed to stave off some of its ravages, but the disease refuses to be cured. We fall under the rule of the English Council of Witches, should we not also get help from that same council?"

"Mother," said Vivienne as she touched Minerva's elbow. "My earth magic is strong. I could take some new initiates who show talent in that area and seed the country anew. Some members of the council would be eager to start new Houses in less crowded conditions."

The three Irish witches gasped with joy and clutched each other. "Thank you," began Shannon.

"No," Minerva cut her off and turned to Vivienne. "I'm surprised you would suggest such a thing. You are vitally needed here, especially in the next year." Her eyes were hard and Vivienne blushed.

"I am sorry for your plight, Sister, but the Council can offer you no help at this time."

The blood drained from Shannon's face and she dropped to her knees, her dress and robes puddling around her, her hands clasped together. Tears streamed down her cheeks openly. "Please, please, Grande Dame, I have watched my own children starve. My people would die of shame instead of empty bellies if they knew I was here to plead our case. This is our last resort. You don't understand the sacrifices we've made."

"Sacrifice?" Minerva's voice rose, along with the color in her cheeks. "You dare to lecture me on sacrifice? You Irish witches seem to have very short memories. It was not so long ago that my own beloved blood sisters went to you and gave their lives trying to save your precious potatoes. Do not presume to lecture me on the subject of sacrifice!"

A murmur surged through the crowd as the party guests whispered behind their hands and fans at the show of emotion from Lady Blackstone. Such a thing was unheard of. Even her daughters glanced at each other with wide eyes and tight lips.

Shannon sank further down, pressing her forehead to the floor. "I meant no disrespect, Sister, we on the Isle are well aware of the sacrifices of the Sortilege line and Blackstone House."

"I find that hard to believe given your temerity, approaching us at such an event with such a request." Even scowling Minerva Sortilege remained beautiful.

"Please, Lady Blackstone," wept the broken water witch. "If there is an ounce of compassion within you, please, help us. We have nowhere else to turn."

"The audacity," gasped Minerva. "You have the nerve to question my love for my sisters in magic? Do you not think it pains me to deny my sisters aid?"

Shannon lifted her tear-streaked face from the floor and shook her head, her mouth opening and closing on no sound. Her sister witches sank to the floor behind her, clutching each other and weeping.

"I have to think of the entire United Kingdom," Minerva's strident voice rose and she raised her right hand, power shimmering around long fingers. "Indeed, given that we are the strongest and most talented witches Mother Earth has seen fit to provide, we must be leaders to the entirety of the world! I have more concerns than just one starving island who cannot manage their resources better than the mundane." Minerva cast forth a wave of magical force with her right hand that shoved all three of the Irish witches into the crowd, knocking over several party guests. Minerva showed no strain at all. She raised her hand again, but Vivienne stepped to her ear and whispered. Lowering her hand, Minerva gave a sharp nod to her eldest, who stepped back into line.

Footmen of the Westerfeld estate came forward and helped the party guests and Irish witches to their feet. The room was utterly silent but for the rustle of fabric. Minerva fixed the invading witches with a frosty glare.

"You would do well to leave now, my Sisters," she said. "Before I become angry and forget my temper. You push me too far and it does your cause no good."

The pale-faced footmen hustled the women from the room with the minimum of courtesy demanded of a witch. The Irish problem would see no resolution this night.

Minerva lifted her chin and schooled her features. "Now, let us continue with the evening's entertainments." She swept up to a profusely sweating Westerfeld in front of the locked door with her daughters in tow. "I do hope you can lighten the mood of the evening, Master Westerfeld." She favored him with an icy smile.

"Indeed," said Westerfeld as he executed a deep bow to the powerful witch. "I do hope that I can amuse you, my lady." He turned and unlocked the pair of gilt doors, sweeping them wide open and leading the guests into a ballroom that glittered in brass, crystal, and mirrors.

About the Author

Michelle D. Sonnier writes dark urban fantasy, steampunk, and anything else that lets her combine the weird and the fantastic in unexpected ways. She even writes horror, although it took her a long time to admit that since she prefers the existential scare over blood and gore. She's published short stories in a variety of print and online venues, and has upcoming projects with eSpec Books and Otter Libris. You can find her on Facebook (Michelle D. Sonnier, The Writer) or at www.michelledsonnier.com. She lives in Maryland with her husband, son, and a variable number of cats. *The Clockwork Witch* is her first full-length novel.

Enchanting Supporters

Alan Danziger
alicat
Amelia Smith
Anders Håkon Gaut
Anonymous
Barb and Carl Kesner
Bec Smith
Becky B
Brad Roberts
Brian Dysart
Brooks Moses
C Foreman
Carol J. Guess
Catherine Gross-Colten
Cathy Green
Chad Bowden
Chris Matosky
Christopher J. Burke
Christy Biggs
Cindy Matera
Craig "Stevo" Stephenson

Craig Hackl
Curtis & Maryrita Steinhour
Dagmar Baumann
Dale A Russell
Dancing Emerald Green Falcon
Daniel Lin
Danielle Wolf
Dave Hermann
David Gian-Cursio
David Lee Summers
      and Kumie Wise
David Perkins
David Zurek
Deborah Hartigan
Debra Lieven
Ed Ellis
Ergo Ojasoo
Eric S. Schaefer
Erik T Johnson
Erin Hudgins
Eryious

Gary Phillips
H Lynnea Johnson
Harald (Germany)
Hrvoje Bukša
Ian Harvey
im just lori
Isaac 'Will It Work' Dansicker
Jakub Narębski
James Rowland
Janice M. Eisen
Jasen Stengel
Jd Michaels
Jeanne Hartley
Jen Myers
Jenn Whitworth
Jenna E. Miller
Jennifer L. Pierce
Jeremy Audet
Joanne Burrows
John "Shadowcat" Ickes
John Fiala
John Idlor
John Kerecz
Jörg Tremmel
Joshua C. Chadd
Judith Waidlich
Kate Deibel
Kelly Pierce
KellyShannon Pierce
Ken "Merlyn" Mencher
Kerry aka Trouble
Kris Mayer
L.E. Custodio
Lark Cunningham
Lewis Phillips
Linda Pierce

Lisa Kruse
Lori and Maurice Forrester
Lorraine J. Anderson
Louise Lowenspets
Mackie
maileguy
Margaret Bumby
Margaret St. John
Mark Carter
Mark Chick
Mark Featherston
Mark Hirschman
Mark Lukens
Megan K. Ward
Megan Real
Melissa Shumake
Mike Bundt
Mike Smith
Mitchell A Johnson
Morgan Hazelwood
Moria Trent
N/A
Nathan Turner
Oliver James Minall
Pam Halter
Paul May
Paul van Oven
Peter D Engebos
Peter Thew
pjk
R.J.H.
Ralf "Sandfox" Sandfuchs
Raven Oak
Regis M. Donovan
RJ Hopkinson
Rob Menaul

Robert Claney
Robert Dallas
Russell Ventimeglia
S Jeff Nelson
Sam Stilwell
Scott Early
Scott Elson
Scott Schaper
Sheepy!
Sheryl R. Hayes
Stephen Ballentine
Stephen Lesnik
Sue Carlson
Svend Andersen

Tanya K.
Tasha Turner
The Archive
Tiffany Hall
Tina M Noe Good
Tory Shade
Tracy 'Rayhne' Fretwell
Trina L Bork
Vespry Family
Victoria Kay Steele
Wes Rist
Wil Bastion
Zoro58